The ICE WHISPERERS

PUFFIN BOOKS

UK | USA | Canada | Ireland | Australia
India | New Zealand | South Africa

Puffin Books is part of the Penguin Random House group of companies
whose addresses can be found at global.penguinrandomhouse.com.

www.penguin.co.uk
www.puffin.co.uk
www.ladybird.co.uk

First published 2021
001

Text design by Mandy Norman
Typeset in Baskerville MT Std
Printed and bound in Great Britain by Clays Ltd, Elcograf S.p.A.

The authorized representative in the EEA is Penguin Random House Ireland,
Morrison Chambers, 32 Nassau Street, Dublin D02 YH68A

CIP catalogue record for this book is available from the British Library

ISBN: 978-0-241-49128-7

All correspondence to:
Puffin Books
Penguin Random House Children's
One Embassy Gardens, 8 Viaduct Gardens, London SW11 7BW

Penguin Random House is committed to a
sustainable future for our business, our readers
and our planet. This book is made from Forest
Stewardship Council® certified paper.

The ICE WHISPERERS

HELENKA STACHERA

Illustrated by
Marco Guadalupi

PUFFIN

For Kat

In the beginning, there was only one world. Everyone had to share it, both the living and the dead. But, as time went on, the dead came to outnumber the living. And so a spirit world was born . . .

PROLOGUE

Northern Siberia, 40,000 years ago

The wind changes direction, veering from the west to the north. Ren-*ya* lifts her face to the breeze and sticks her tongue out into the drifting snow. She tastes pine resin, the mineral tang of ice, the day-old musk of elk. But something else is carried to her on the wind from far away, something that burns the back of her throat. She recognizes the faint, sharp flavour: *white-eyes*.

Ren-*ya* follows the flavour upwind. Her snowshoes make her fly and she hardly leaves a mark as she runs over the deep white drifts. She positions herself at the top of a ridge. Crouched behind a stand of gnarled spruce trees, she waits. The morning passes and at last the invaders appear: hunched figures emerging from a

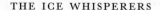

ghostly mist. Ren-*ya* watches from her hiding place as they approach, counts them as they pass beneath her. Ten shrouded warriors lead the way, their heads feathered under their hoods. Then come the followers, strung out in a line behind them, walking in twos. Each pair hefts long wooden poles between them that creak with the weight of bison hides, water sacs, the dangling limbs of a recent kill. They slog on, heads bowed.

From time to time, one of them looks up and she catches sight of their eyes. They are milk-white, and, in the centre, each has a darting circle that is brown or grey, sometimes blue. So different to the wide black eyes of Ren-*ya*'s people, the Last.

Animals travel with the *white-eyes*. They look something like wolves, only they lick the humans' hands and trot at their heels as no wolf

ever would. One draws level with Ren-*ya*, no more than twenty strides away. It lifts its blunt snout and snuffs at the air, but Ren-*ya* has deadened her odour with juniper and not even a cave bear could sniff her out.

She follows them all day and in the late afternoon, when the sun skims the tops of the trees, they stop and make camp. Ren-*ya* watches as they gather firewood, erect the wooden poles and cover them with the bison skins. She listens to their chatter, although she cannot understand the sounds they make. They are as alien to her as their animals are to wolves, yet she has heard them laugh and even sing. She is both fascinated and afraid. Part of her would like to step out, show herself, but, although Ren-*ya* is not yet grown, she knows they would skewer her before she had a chance to raise her empty hand in peace.

As darkness falls, she slips away and runs through the night.

She is still some way from home when she sees her mother, Nagar, coming towards her in the creeping light of dawn. Ren-*ya* runs and throws her arms round her, too breathless to even say her mother's name.

'Where have you been?' Nagar says. Then, when she sees Ren-*ya*'s face, 'What has happened?'

'*White-eyes.*'

Her mother presses her hand to her heart and calls on the ancestors for help. 'Come,' she says. 'We must tell Hebera at once.'

They hurry over the mounting snowdrifts and run through forest trees hung with ice, every breath blooming in the air like a puff of smoke. Eventually, they cross the wide, frozen river and reach the caves. At the entrance, Ren-*ya* blows the horn and the Last troop out of the dark tunnels and sit round the meeting fire. They wait in silence for their leader, the shaman Hebera.

She emerges from the caves, an old woman with a face so still and set it might be hewn from rock. A black-feathered bird sits on her shoulder and she wears the splayed wings of a vulture for a cloak.

'What news, Ren-*ya*?' Hebera says.

'The *white-eyes* are coming.'

'How far?'

'A night of running.'

Ren-*ya* can taste the sour-milk flavour of fear that seeps from the skin of her people. A generation has gone by since the *white-eyes* first appeared on the plains. Back then, the Last sent a handful of warriors to welcome them. They took gifts of meat and berries, the tail

So Ren-*ya* and her people leave their home and travel north to the foothills of the snowy mountains. There they light another great fire and chant through day and night. But Malor has been whispering to the people, questioning what Nagar says, and when Hebera asks who will be the first to go, no one steps forward.

Ren-*ya* is afraid too, but she knows her mother does not lie. 'I will go first,' she says.

Ren-*ya* lies down on the ice and the Last cover her with snow, leaving only her face open to the sky. Her mother puts the glittering stone under Ren-*ya*'s tongue. 'Sleep and have no fear,' she says. 'The ancestors will carry you safely to the spirit world.'

Nagar watches over her daughter until she sleeps. Then she takes the crystal orb from Ren-*ya*'s bloodless lips and covers her face with snow. Nagar lays the totem in the mouths of the Last and, one by one, they fall asleep.

Snow upon snow falls on their bodies and the Last are buried deep.

For a long time, there is nothing but snow and ice, nothing but the cold. Then, at last, a change comes.

The earth warms.

The glaciers begin to melt.

PART ONE

POLAND, 1910

THE TASTE OF TREACHERY

Bela was woken by shouting – 'Up there! Look! Someone, help her!' – and, when she came to, she found herself standing high above the cobbled streets of Kraków, her toes curled over the edge of the steeply sloping roof.

For a moment, shock froze her to the spot. Far below, a crowd had gathered and, as Bela swayed over the yawning void, someone cried out, 'She's going to fall!'

Bela took a tiny step back from the edge, her heart hammering in her chest. In the houses on the other side of the street, people threw open their windows, hanging out as far as they dared to get a better view. Bela heard their terrified gasps as she dropped to a crouch on the tiles.

Don't look down, Bela told herself. But it was a humid summer night and half the city seemed to be out on the streets. She couldn't help catching glimpses of the people below, their upturned faces lit by the gas lamps: some horrified, others eager.

A voice came out of the darkness behind her. 'Oh my goodness! Bela! What are you doing out there?'

Bela slowly turned her head. The housekeeper and one of the maids were only a few feet away, leaning from the window of Bela's attic bedroom.

'Be careful!' They stretched their arms out, ready to grab her as, inch by inch, Bela crawled across the tiles towards them. A great cry of relief and disappointment rose up from the street as Bela climbed back through the window to safety.

'What on earth did you think you were doing?' the housekeeper said once she and the maid had got Bela back into bed. 'You could've been killed!'

Bela's body was still trembling. 'I . . . I was dreaming,' she managed to stammer out.

'About what?'

It was difficult to piece it all together. She remembered a black-and-white bird tapping at her window, and before that there had been someone standing at the bottom of her bed. A woman with auburn hair, just like Bela's.

'I was dreaming about my mother,' she said.

'Oh.' The housekeeper exchanged a knowing look with the maid and quickly changed the subject. 'Here.' She handed Bela a glass. 'Have something to drink.'

Bela gulped the water down, but it didn't wash away the cloying flavour of ashes that clung to her tongue. The woman in her dream had tasted of it.

'I dreamed my mother was dead.'

Three days later, Bela was summoned to the library where Great-aunt Olga was waiting for her. On the couch opposite was Olga's lawyer, Zabrowski. He sat motionless, his face and clothes so lacking in colour that he seemed more like an ageing sepia photograph than a living human being.

'Ah, Bela, there you are.' Olga got to her feet and smoothed the wrinkles from the fine silk of her skirt. 'Please sit down.'

Bela lowered herself cautiously into one of the plump velvet armchairs. She could tell from the sharp taste that hung in the air that something was wrong. Was she about to get another dressing-down for the sleepwalking incident? Olga had been furious, especially when she realized the whole street had witnessed Bela's 'shameful escapade'.

'I'm afraid I have some bad news.' Olga arranged

her face into what she clearly considered a sympathetic expression. 'I received a telegram today from your uncle in Siberia.'

Bela held her breath. Her mother lived in Uncle Viktor's house and there could only be one reason for him to send a telegram.

'I'm sorry to inform you,' Olga continued, 'that your mother has passed away.'

Since the dream, Bela had felt as if a great weight was hanging over her, and now Olga's cold words fell into her heart like stones. 'When?' she said.

'Three nights ago.'

Three nights? But that was when she woke up on the roof. She must have been dreaming of her mother at the very moment of her death. Bela remembered the silent figure who'd stood at the bottom of her bed. It had been more than a nightmare: it had been a visitation.

'Of course, it's very sad,' Aunt Olga continued. 'Although one can't help feeling that it may all be for the best.'

Bela couldn't believe what she was hearing. 'What do you mean, "for the best"?'

Olga's face took on a pained expression. 'I should have thought the benefits were obvious, in view of your mother's —' she raised a handkerchief to her mouth to smother the offending word — '*illness.*'

Bela's mouth flooded with the sick taste of shame. Her mother had suffered from a malady that was spoken of in whispers, behind closed doors, a condition that could not be mentioned in polite society. It was one thing to break a leg or catch the measles, quite another to be 'deranged'. The shame of it seeped out of the afflicted person and attached itself to their friends and relatives. Bela knew Olga was expecting her to end up the same way, to inherit the curse of madness from her mother.

Once Olga had dispensed a few more bland words of comfort, Bela was sent off to bed. But she had hardly made it up the first flight of stairs to her room before a syrupy taste escaped from a crack in the library door, floated up through the dusty air of the old house and reached Bela. She leaned over the banister and drew a long breath into her lungs. The flavour was one she'd often tasted on her aunt, but never as strongly as this. It seemed as sweet as sugar dust, but soon turned to bitterness on the back of her tongue. It was the taste of treachery.

Bela glided silently back down the stairs to the library and peered in. She could see Great-aunt Olga and Zabrowski, their heads together over a large mahogany desk.

'What are the terms?' Olga was saying.

Zabrowski replied in a voice as dry as his legal papers. 'Professor Novak has made a very generous offer. As his ward, she'll inherit Wilder House on his death.'

Olga huffed. 'What good is that to me?'

Zabrowski acknowledged his client's concern with a small bow. 'He promises to make a large cash payment for your trouble, but only if you send her to him in Siberia straight away.'

It was all Bela could do to remain hidden and quiet. How dare her aunt sell her off as if she was one of her possessions?

But Olga had no such misgivings. 'Well, that's settled then,' she said. 'After all, she can't stay here, especially after that incident on the roof. I dread to think how many people saw her.' Olga picked up a pen. 'Where should I sign?'

Zabrowski cleared his throat politely. 'There is just the matter of the girl's welfare to consider. Doesn't it

strike you as odd that Professor Novak is asking for the girl now? And why the urgency? He's shown no interest in her before, but now her mother's dead he immediately sends for her.'

Olga shrugged. 'As regards her welfare, I rather think I've done my bit. After all, I've fed and clothed the child since her father went off on his foolhardy expedition and disappeared.'

Zabrowski nodded. 'Indeed, madam. But the girl is what, thirteen? She'll be married off in a few years.'

Olga snorted. 'You men have no idea about these matters. Who would want to marry her?' She lowered her voice to a whisper. 'She won't be able to hide that hideous mark on her hand forever.'

Bela felt a stab of humiliation. The 'hideous mark' was a tattoo that Bela's mother had scratched into the palm of her hand when she was a baby. Olga said it was a disgrace and made Bela wear gloves to hide it.

Bela's great-aunt continued to list the reasons no one would ever want to marry her niece. 'The child is most disagreeable,' she said. 'And far too quick to give her opinion. Worse, she has no money, no property, nothing to make up for her . . . drawbacks.'

Zabrowski raised an eyebrow. 'You mean the mother?'

'Of course I mean the mother! Who else? The

woman was an *illiterate tribeswoman*. A lunatic. Who would want to marry into that? Especially now the girl is going the same way . . .' She sighed and in that exhaled breath, Bela caught the vinegary taste of her aunt's disapproval. 'It's for her own good. For the sake of the family's reputation, sacrifices must be made.' She leaned over the papers that lay on the desk and signed Bela away with a flourish.

Outside the library door, Bela closed her hands into fists. She had no choice about where she was sent, but of one thing she was certain: she would be nobody's sacrifice.

BLACK EYES

The next day, Bela's bag was packed and she was put on the train to Siberia in a first-class compartment. Aunt Olga complained bitterly about the expense, but one of her many acquaintances might be at the station, or on the train itself, and it would tarnish the family's reputation if Bela was seen travelling in second class.

Bela's compartment was small but well appointed with a couch that, each evening, was made up into a narrow bed. There was a triangular sink in the corner, with a mirror above, where Bela washed her face and combed her hair. Her meals were taken in the dining car, where as many as five elaborate courses were served on gilt-edged china and eaten with silver-plated cutlery.

Although the train was grand, it was slow. There

were endless stops at out-of-the-way stations and it often came to a complete standstill during the night. The carriages dawdled out of Kraków and trundled through the late golden summer of the Polish countryside. They crossed the wide expanses of Russia, going ever further north and east, idling towards the plains and forests of Siberia. The journey was expected to take as long as four weeks, and Bela spent the endless days and nights turning over in her mind everything that had happened.

Although she had no choice about leaving Kraków, she was glad to get away from her great-aunt. At least her uncle seemed to want her. An image of Olga's pinched face came into Bela's mind as she remembered the hateful things she'd said about her. *That hideous mark* . . . She tugged off the glove on her left hand and peered at the tattoo on her palm. It was a series of dots in the shape of a triangle, a clan mark belonging to her mother's nomadic tribe. Bela hated it. She had spent many hours trying to wash it off before she finally understood that soap and water would never erase it. The tattoo had meant she couldn't go to school or have friends, Olga had said, in case someone saw it. It was a shameful thing, a sign of Bela's uncivilized parentage.

The tattoo wasn't the only thing that made Bela different. She had a heightened sense of taste and lived in a world full of an endless variety of vivid flavours.

While other people looked and listened to each other, Bela *tasted* what people were thinking and feeling. She never talked to anyone about it. Like the tattoo, it was something she'd learned to hide.

Bela opened her bag and took out a framed picture. The photograph had been taken in Siberia, just before Bela was born. It was spring and her parents were standing by an open window, her father's hand held protectively over her mother's rounded belly. At the last moment, Bela's mother must have turned her head to look at something outside, for all that could be seen of her face was a black-and-white smudge.

Bela thought they must have been an unlikely couple: a scientist and an uneducated tribeswoman. She didn't remember either of them, but she missed them nonetheless. Olga used to say you couldn't miss what you'd never had, but Bela knew you could. It was a hunger that was never satisfied. A longing that, when it came upon her, flooded her mouth with the flavour of stagnant water – the unbearable taste of loss.

Your parents were part of what made you who you were. Without them, wouldn't there always be a piece missing? And yet she felt strangely disconnected from the pain of her mother's death since she had already been lost to Bela so long ago.

In the background of the photograph, there was a cabinet full of the ancient artefacts her father had dug up. She wondered what could have happened to him. Olga said he had gone off on one of his expeditions and disappeared. But how? And why was his body never found? Olga had always dismissed her questions and said it was no use crying over spilled milk. But now Bela hoped to find the answers in Siberia, in the house where she herself had been born. Wilder House, where her father had grown up and where her sick mother had lived until her death.

Bela traced the smudge of her mother's face with her fingertip. Why did she send Bela away to live with Olga when she was only a baby? Why had she never asked to see her since? Bela had been waiting her whole life for her mother to get better, to call her back to Siberia, but now she never would.

She found herself searching the image for any sign of her mother's ailment. However hard she tried, she couldn't ignore the question that was always at the front of her mind: *Will I end up mad like her?* Maybe the sleepwalking was a sign of worse to come. The thought left Bela with a pain in the pit of her stomach that felt like hunger. She picked up the discarded glove and tugged it back on, concealing the tattoo that marked her out as her mother's daughter.

She must look to the future now, and she hoped to find a home with her uncle. After all, he was her father's brother, and a scientist. Bela loved to read and learn, so they might have a lot in common. When she thought of her new home, the flavour of fresh pine needles settled on her tongue. She had left Siberia as a baby, so she didn't remember Wilder House, but she imagined a warm and welcoming haven set in the midst of an icy land. Above all, she hoped that in Siberia she would find a family.

The train was finally approaching Bela's destination, a small town deep in the heart of the taiga, not far from the cold embrace of the Arctic Circle. She'd left Kraków in the heat of summer, but here autumn was preparing to turn to winter. The nearer she got, the more on edge she became. She found it difficult to sleep, and when she did manage to drop off, her dreams were disturbing and left her just as tired as if she'd had no sleep at all.

On Bela's final night on the train, she had a terrible nightmare. She dreamed there was a tapping at the door of her compartment, but when she opened it no one was there. She looked out into the corridor and caught a glimpse of a woman hurrying away before the door at the end of the carriage slid shut behind her. Bela went after her, but by the time she got through to the next carriage, the woman was disappearing into the one after that. Bela was filled with terror at the thought of never catching up with her. But it didn't matter how fast she ran – the woman was always one carriage ahead.

'Stop!' she shouted after her. 'Please! I just want to see your face.'

The woman stopped, and when she turned round Bela felt she was looking in a mirror: she had the very same heart-shaped face and auburn hair.

But it was the woman's eyes that seemed to stop her heart. They were entirely black.

WILDER HOUSE

The next morning Bela arrived at the station in Siberia and climbed down from the train on to the platform.

A man approached. He removed his mink-fur hat and made a small bow. 'Miss Novak? Welcome to Siberia. I am Doctor Krol, until lately your mother's personal physician.' Everything about him was smooth – his voice, his skin, his slicked-back hair. 'May I express my deepest condolences for your loss?' He sounded sincere, but the oily flavour that surrounded him told Bela he didn't mean a word of it.

'Where's my uncle?'

The doctor gave her a practised smile. 'The professor wanted to be here to meet you, but unfortunately he's away.'

Krol picked up her bag and led her out of the station, where a carriage was waiting. 'This is Arno,' he said, nodding to the driver.

A scarf covered the lower half of the driver's face and Bela could only see his narrow grey eyes. The man didn't even blink.

'Arno doesn't speak Polish,' Krol explained.

Bela shrugged. 'I can speak Russian.'

'He has no Russian either, I'm afraid.'

Arno continued to stare straight ahead, the reins in one hand, a short whip in the other. He looked as if he had no thoughts in his head at all. But there were many flavours hanging in the air around him. Bela noted a taste like the powdery mould on a rind of cheese; behind his quiet mask, the man was full of regret.

The two black horses hitched to the coach were just as quiet and stood stock-still, their breath clouding in the cold air. They were fine animals with glossy coats and plumes of feathers at their foreheads. Bela reached out to touch the neck of the nearest and it jerked its head up, its eyes whitening behind the blinkers.

Krol took hold of her elbow. 'Be careful. They're not pets.'

Bela wrested her arm away. 'And nor am I,' she said, climbing into the carriage.

He smiled, showing even white teeth. 'I have business in town tonight, but Arno will make sure you reach the house safely.' He handed in her bag, rapped on the door and the carriage lurched off.

Soon they left the town behind and the horses drew them deep into the quiet gloom of the forest. The road here was unmade and bumpy. It wound between tall trees that grew so close together their feet were planted in darkness.

They travelled through the afternoon, never once leaving the vast forest, and it was evening by the time the carriage drove in through two high iron gates and entered the estate. The sun had dipped behind the distant mountains, leaving crimson trails smeared across the sky. Bela pressed her face to the window, keen to see the place where her parents had lived – and where she'd been born.

Through the trees, she caught glimpses of Wilder House, but it was not the idyllic place she had imagined. Its many windows reflected snatches of the sunset and blazed blood-red. One side of the house was clad in scaffolding right up to the roof, which gleamed in the twilight, the slate tiles like the overlapping scales of a great black snake.

It wasn't just the look of the place that was daunting. Bela pulled down the window and tasted the cold air that drifted between the tall trees. It was too faint to be sure, but the flavour on her tongue was slippery, like deceit.

The carriage disturbed a black-and-white bird roosting in the branches of a tall tree and Bela watched it flap away, its grating cries gradually fading as it flew off into the night. For a moment, she could have sworn it was the same magpie who'd been tapping on her window in her dreams, but she quickly dismissed the idea. She told herself she was just unsettled by the sight and taste of her new home, but she was careful to whisper a salute to the bird, to avert the bad luck of seeing a single magpie.

Arno drew the carriage up in front of the house. He helped Bela step down and carried her bag to the front door, where a striking woman was waiting to greet her. Although she was young, her hair was white. It was swept up and back, showing off the fine angular lines of her face. Her brows and lashes were also white, which made her pale blue eyes seem frosted with snow.

'You must be Bela,' she said. 'Welcome to Wilder House.'

She put an arm round Bela's shoulders and guided her into a long hallway. The stone floor was made of alternating black and white tiles, like a chessboard, and the walls were covered in the gold-framed portraits of

people who must have been dead for hundreds of years. Their cold, painted eyes looked down on Bela in a way that did nothing to dispel her unease.

The woman led her on through an arched doorway and up a broad staircase. 'I expect you're tired,' she said. 'I'll take you to your room straight away.' She paused halfway up the first flight. 'Listen to me twittering on, and we haven't even been introduced! I'm Eva Balinsky, the professor's personal assistant. If you need anything, I'm the one to ask.'

Her words were friendly enough, but an acrid taste in the air told Bela she wasn't completely welcome in that house.

Eva led her to the top floor. 'This is your room.'

Inside, there was a chest of drawers with a mirror over it and a ceramic jug and bowl. Bela's bag had already been brought up and was placed on top of an iron bedstead. The walls were whitewashed and there were no paintings or pictures at all.

Eva motioned for Bela to go in. 'I expect you'd like to rest. I've had some supper brought up.' She pointed to a table where a tray had been laid out with slices of bread and butter and cheese. 'If you want anything else, ring the bell. One of the maids will see to it.'

When Bela had eaten and the house was quiet, she went to the window and looked out. There was a small balcony with a view over the drive at the front. The moon was up now and she could see the tall cedars that were closest to the house and, past those, the woods. Further away still, beyond the walls of the estate, a seemingly endless forest stretched away into the distance. As she stood there, she heard the fluting call of an unseen night bird, answered by the eerie scream of a fox. It suddenly struck Bela how wild this place was – and how far the estate was from the nearest town.

The thought of being in the middle of nowhere made her uneasy. Why did her uncle suddenly want her here? Even Zabrowski, Olga's desiccated lawyer, had thought there was something a bit odd about it.

She unpacked the photograph of her parents and put it carefully on the bedside table. *My mother was alive, here in this house, less than a month ago.*

Bela went out of her room and stood at the top of the stairs. She breathed deeply, drawing in the smells and flavours of the unknown house. If she was hoping for some faint remnant of her mother, she was disappointed. Now she was alone, there was only a strong antiseptic taste on the air. Every human emotion had been mopped up with disinfectant and sluiced away.

THE LION-HEADED MAN

The next morning, when Bela went down for breakfast, Eva was already in the dining room, drinking coffee. She got up and served Bela some coddled eggs from a silver tureen. She said that the professor had returned from his business trip, but wouldn't be able to see Bela until that afternoon.

'He's always so busy,' she said. 'But after breakfast, I'll show you around if you like.' She explained that the house was divided in two. 'The east wing has been renovated, but apart from the professor's quarters the west wing hasn't been touched. You might've noticed the scaffolding when you arrived? It's a danger and I must ask you to stay away from the west wing.'

At that moment, Dr Krol came in and served

himself some breakfast. Bela had instantly disliked the man, but he'd been her mother's doctor and she needed to know how and why she had died. She forced herself to engage him in a few words of polite small talk before turning the conversation to her mother's illness.

'I was wondering,' she said, 'what exactly was wrong with my mother?'

'A very delicate subject,' Krol said as he stirred sugar into his coffee. 'Hardly something to discuss with ladies present, and certainly not over breakfast.'

Bela was well used to a particular kind of man denying her information purely on the grounds that she was female. 'Well,' she said, 'I don't mind, and if Eva has no objections?'

Krol glanced over at Eva, no doubt for support, but Eva stared resolutely into her coffee cup. He gave Bela one of his smooth smiles. 'Your mother had an acute case of female hysteria.'

'Oh? What's that?'

Krol leaned forward, warming to his subject. 'It's a common disease among women, no doubt caused by the markedly smaller structures present in the female brain.'

Eva glanced up from her coffee, a thin smile on her face. 'Doctor Krol is a phrenologist, Bela. He believes diseases of the mind can be diagnosed according to the lumps and bumps on a person's head. Isn't that right, Doctor?'

Krol's face took on a pinched expression. 'Women's skulls are markedly smaller than those of men, and it's no surprise to me that when we look about the world we find no great female scientists or artists. Women just don't have the brains for it.'

Bela's breathing quickened. She was finding it difficult to hide her outrage and she wasn't the only one; the air in the room was thick with the burnt-hair taste of Eva's anger, yet when she spoke her voice was icy cold. 'An interesting theory, Doctor. But I should've thought it more likely due to a lack of education and opportunity.'

'I agree,' Bela said. 'When are women given the chance to show what they can do?'

Dr Krol cleared his throat and placed his cup carefully in its saucer. 'With the greatest respect, Miss Novak, you would do well to ignore Miss Balinsky's amateur opinions. I am a doctor with much experience

in these matters.' He leaned forward, and the oily flavour that seeped from his pores became almost unbearable. 'After all,' he said, 'I was your mother's personal physician for many years.'

Bela felt the flush of shame creep up her neck. She knew exactly what the doctor was doing. He didn't like his ideas being questioned, and was trying to shut her up by reminding everyone that her mother was a madwoman.

Bela took a leaf out of the doctor's book and covered her anger with a smile. 'Tell me, Doctor, for how long was my mother a patient of yours?'

'Twelve years.'

Bela pretended to think for a moment. 'But despite your "expertise", in all that time you were unable to cure her?'

Dr Krol's nostrils flared as he gazed at Bela. 'It wasn't for lack of trying – I can assure you of that. We might be in the backwoods out here, but I have recourse to all the modern methods: sedative drugs, enforced

immobility, electric-shock therapy, ice baths.' His smile grew and Bela could tell he was enjoying listing his macabre treatments. 'We doctors do what we can, but madness is so often inherited.' He looked pointedly at Bela. 'It's in the blood, passed down from father to son, mother to –'

Suddenly Eva got up. 'I think we'll leave it there, Doctor Krol. Bela and I have much to do. Good day.' She took hold of Bela's arm and swept her from the room.

Once they were outside, Eva said, 'I'm sorry you had to hear all that.'

She spoke calmly, but Bela could still taste the fire of the feelings she was hiding. 'You don't approve of Doctor Krol's methods, do you?'

'The way he paints it, one could imagine that being a woman was a disease in itself.'

They smiled together at the joke, and Bela sensed that some of the hostility she'd tasted on Eva when she'd arrived was melting.

'I shouldn't let him rile me,' Eva continued. 'He has his work and I have mine. Only –'

'Only what?'

Eva shook her head. 'It doesn't matter. Come, I'll show you your father's study. I expect you'd like to see it?'

She led the way upstairs and unlocked a door at the top. The room was stuffed with books that filled the study with the comforting aroma of old paper. There was a large desk covered in framed photographs and Bela went over and picked one up.

Eva stood behind her. 'That's your father collecting his diploma. He looks so young.' She handed another picture to Bela. 'Look at this. The two brothers together.'

Bela peered at the picture. Her father was hardly more than a baby. He was trussed up in a little velvet suit with a lace collar and looked into the camera with a puzzled expression. Viktor was years older and loomed over his brother, staring down at him with narrowed eyes.

'Did they get on as children?' Bela asked.

Eva shrugged. 'I don't think they spent much time together. Apparently, the professor went off to boarding school not long after this photograph was taken.'

Bela moved over to a wide chest with narrow drawers. 'What's in here?'

'Artefacts. The pieces your father found. Would you like to have a look?' Eva slid the top drawer out.

Inside were many pieces of jagged stone carefully arranged in rows. The mysterious mineral flavour that escaped from the drawer quickened Bela's heartbeat. It was a new flavour, and quite intoxicating.

'These are cutting tools,' Eva said. 'All thousands of years old.'

Bela picked one up. 'Gulf of Ob, May 1890,' she said, reading the label.

Eva looked pleased. 'I spent ages working out what artefacts were found at which site and when. Your father's system might've made sense to him, but it wasn't obvious to anyone else.'

'What do *you* think happened to him?'

Eva cast her eyes down. 'The professor says he disappeared during a snowstorm, but what happened to him after that no one knows.'

'The professor was there?'

Eva nodded. 'He was helping your father with his work.' For a moment, Eva was silent and then she said, 'Anyway, some of the artefacts are quite extraordinary.' She opened another drawer, took out a carved figure made of white stone and handed it to Bela. 'Look at this.'

Bela turned the piece in her hand. The same intriguing taste emanated from it: a subtle earthiness mixed with a flavour that prickled on her tongue like tarnished metal. She felt as if she was catching the fleeting taste of an ancient power. 'Is it a man or a lion?'

Eva smiled. 'Both. It has the body of a man and the head of a lion. Your father thought it a ceremonial piece to help hunters catch their prey.' Eva's voice rose with excitement, and when Bela turned to look at her, her pale cheeks were flushed. 'I went to many of your father's talks. Doctor Novak was one of the only academics who let women attend his public lectures and I didn't miss one. He was such an engaging speaker. You could tell he was truly passionate about his subject.'

Bela stared at her. 'How did you end up working for him?'

'I wrote to your father, expressing my enthusiasm, and he replied, offering me a job. He said he was looking for a secretary, someone to oversee his finds. Of course, I jumped at the chance.' She looked round the room. 'I hope I've done him justice. Nothing has been touched. Everything is exactly as he left it . . .'

'But now you work for the professor?'

'Well, yes, after your father disappeared, Professor Novak asked me to stay on. He wanted to continue your father's work, and no one knows his finds better than I do.' Eva indicated the rows of leather-bound books on the shelves. 'Everything your father wrote is out of print now, which is a shame because his ideas deserve an audience.' She pulled a book off the shelf. 'This is one of his handwritten journals. He kept detailed notes about every expedition he went on.'

'Can I take it? To read later?'

Eva smiled and handed it to her. 'Of course. Now, is there anything else you'd like to see?' As soon as she said it, Eva must have realized what Bela would ask because her face fell.

'Will you show me where my mother is buried?'

The graveyard was a little cordoned-off plot in the woods beside the house. Bela's mother's grave was the newest one and the mounded earth was still bare. A rough wooden cross had been erected, Eva said, until a proper stone one could be brought from town. But for Bela it felt like an insult, the careless, barren grave a sign of the family's disregard for her mother. Even the family name seemed to have been omitted. The cross read only NAGAR, and the date, 11 AUGUST 1910.

'Why just Nagar?' Bela asked. 'Why not Nagar Novak?'

Eva cleared her throat. 'Your parents weren't legally married. You see, your mother insisted on a tribal ceremony.'

'What did that involve?'

'An exchange of blood. It was a bit of a scandal at the time. None of your father's family attended.' For a moment, Eva's gaze rested on Bela's face. 'You look a lot like him, you know. When you were born, he was so happy. He loved you a great deal.'

A sudden urge to cry took Bela by surprise and she turned away. 'What was she like, my mother?'

'She was . . . different. I'd never met anyone like her.'

'Mad, you mean?'

Eva shrugged. 'I leave the diagnosing to Doctor Krol.'

'Did my father think she was mad?'

'No!' Eva looked shocked. 'It was only after his disappearance that the professor thought it necessary to employ Doctor Krol. Your father would never have allowed her to be locked up.'

Bela was horrified. 'What do you mean, "locked up"?'

'The professor and Doctor Krol said your mother needed complete rest and quiet. They kept her in a room in the west wing, beyond the professor's quarters.'

Dr Krol . . . the thought of him made Bela shudder. 'Did she suffer much?'

Eva shrugged again. 'Once she was under the doctor's care, none of us saw her.'

'Maybe I could've helped,' Bela said sadly. 'If only she hadn't sent me away.'

'Sent you away? Who told you that?'

'Aunt Olga.'

Eva shook her head. 'It was your father's family who sent you to Kraków.'

Bela's heart started beating hard. She imagined her mother, helpless, locked in that house. She kneeled down by the grave, wondering what other half-truths and lies she'd been told before she learned to recognize their oily taste.

Eva looked back towards the house. 'I expect you'd like to be alone for a while. I'll come and find you in time for your appointment with the professor.'

When she'd gone, Bela turned back to the grave. She tried to imagine what it must've been like. Twelve long years under the care of Dr Krol. She shuddered as she remembered his list of treatments; his so-called cures were surely worse than the disease itself. She looked back to the great house. For her mother, it had been a prison.

She'd thought that coming here and finding out about her parents would heal the emptiness inside her. But everything she'd believed had turned out to be a lie, and the details of her father's life and her mother's death were like salt poured on the wound.

Bela turned back to the mound of earth. 'I wish I'd known you,' she said.

She stripped off the glove that hid her tattoo and laid it on the grave, like a flower.

THE PROFESSOR'S LABORATORY

That afternoon, Eva took Bela to the professor's study. She led her to a polished mahogany desk in front of a tall window and pulled out a chair. 'I'll see you later,' Eva said. 'I'm sure he won't be long.'

When Eva had gone, Bela looked around, wondering what kind of person her uncle would prove to be. Everything on his desk was neatly arranged: the books and papers placed in orderly piles, the pens lined up precisely with the blotting pad. She couldn't identify the faint flavour that hung in the room, but it tasted unpleasant, as if something had long ago rotted away. She'd started her journey to Siberia with high hopes that her uncle would be a kindred spirit, but now that Bela had seen something of what went on in his house she knew how unlikely that was.

Bela sighed and gazed round the room. On one side, there was a cabinet full of guns. She could see the long barrels of hunting rifles, the dull metallic gleam of revolvers. On the other side stood a row of towering shelves stacked with brimming specimen jars.

A dusty ray of sunshine fought through the gloom, illuminating the murky contents, and Bela got up to have a look. Some containers held strange, colourless creatures floating in liquid, while one shelf was labelled EUROPEAN PARASITES over a row of jarred liver flukes. Bela screwed up her face at a bottle containing a clump of long white worms, all twisted together like overcooked spaghetti. On the lower shelf she was shocked to find a number of preserved brains of different sizes, some whole, some cut in cross-section. Up close, Bela could see white threads, like mould, clinging to the grey maze.

She nearly cried out when someone cleared their throat behind her and she turned to see a man in the doorway. He was almost entirely grey, from his tweed jacket to his hair, to his neat, pointed beard. Even his skin had a powdery greyish pallor. Only his eyes were blue and veined with red, as if he hadn't slept for days.

'Uncle Viktor?'

He came into the room and closed the door. 'Did I startle you?'

'A little.'

'I see you're interested in my collection.' His lips curled into a lopsided smile. 'I hope you're not alarmed. Some people find them quite off-putting.'

They stood looking at each other silently in the gloom.

The professor went behind the desk and sat down in a leather-backed chair. 'I hope your journey here was comfortable.' He motioned for Bela to sit down too. 'Eva has made you welcome, I trust?'

'She's been very kind . . . She happened to mention that you were on my father's last expedition.' Bela knew it was rude to bring up the subject of her father so soon, but the questions had been burning inside her for so long, she couldn't wait a moment longer.

The professor's mouth twitched. 'It was very sad.'

'What happened?'

'Who knows? All I can tell you is that there was a snowstorm overnight, and in the morning Sacha was gone.

'We looked everywhere,' he continued. 'There was no sign of him. He'd disappeared.'

An oily taste coated the back of Bela's tongue and any dutiful respect she'd felt for her uncle drained away at his lie. 'I see.'

'I wish I could tell you more. All I can think is that

he wandered off in the night and got lost. Of course, I blame myself.' He smiled in a way that told Bela he didn't blame himself one bit.

There was a tense silence until Bela said, 'I was wondering, Uncle, why did you send for me?'

'You will see that I'm unmarried and have no heir. As my ward, you will learn to run the estate and, in time, inherit it . . .' The professor continued with what sounded to Bela like a carefully prepared answer.

As he spoke, his hand went to his throat and her gaze was drawn to a gleaming white orb that hung round his neck. The stone seemed to pull all the brightness in the room towards it. Perhaps it was because the crystal stood out against the greyness of her uncle's face and clothes, or because, as Bela imagined, it shone with a light that was all its own. The orb was translucent, with swirling golden points of light that seemed to shift and turn. She couldn't take her eyes off it. The stone glittered enticingly at her, but when the professor saw her looking, he tucked it out of sight.

Just then there was a strange high-pitched shriek and Bela spun round in her seat. The sound seemed to be coming from the other side of the room and Bela's gaze flicked to the shelves with their rows of jars, half expecting one of the grisly specimens to have come to life.

The high-pitched mewling came again. 'What's that?' Bela said.

The professor got up. 'Come along. I'll show you.'

He led her through a door behind the cabinets. 'This is my laboratory,' he said.

Bela glanced around, taking in the marble-topped benches, the stacks of Petri dishes and flasks, the deep ceramic basin with its dripping tap. The shelves here were also crammed with specimens, only these were still alive.

There was a whole wall of small wire cages, each with a twitching pink-eyed rat inside. In the middle of the lab, all by itself, stood a large glass dome on a pedestal. Inside the dome was another rat. It hissed at her approach.

'What is this?' Bela looked over at her uncle who was leaning in the doorway, an amused expression on his face.

'One of my experiments.' He came over and peered through the glass at the rat. 'Interesting, don't you think?'

'What kind of experiment?' Bela asked.

'One that explores the effects of sleep deprivation.'

The flavour that Bela had noticed on entering the

study was now so intense it was like another presence in the room. It must be the professor's malice that thickened the air between them. The taste was sickeningly sweet, like an overripe melon left to rot. It turned her stomach and she longed to scrape it from her tongue.

When she managed to speak, Bela's voice sounded as if it came from far away. 'Why would you do this?'

'Knowledge, my dear. All the achievements, all the scientific understanding we have accumulated come from experiments like these.' He peered into the glass dome. 'Of course, it's regrettable that the experiment causes suffering.'

'It's cruel,' Bela said. 'Cruel and heartless.'

The professor didn't look angry; he just nodded. 'I can see why it might seem that way to an ignorant child, but without pain there would be no discovery, no progress . . . And anyway, it's only a rat.'

After that, Bela didn't say another word. It was all so far from the studious exploration of nature she had imagined she might share with her uncle. The professor continued to explain his experiments, but Bela wasn't listening any more. Instead, she stared at his bleak face, at the grey shadows beneath his eyes and in the hollows of his sunken cheeks. Her uncle smiled often as he talked, but it wasn't a friendly smile. His lips were always pressed firmly together and she never saw his teeth.

·   At last the lecture was over and he led Bela out of the laboratory back to his study. 'I will see you at dinner,' he said, closing the door on her.

Bela made her way along the corridor. There were hot tears gathering behind her eyes, a hard lump burning in her throat. She quickened her pace. No, she would not cry.

In the stairwell, she almost ran into Eva. 'Bela? What's the matter?' She caught her by the arm. 'Are you all right?'

'Have you seen what he does in that laboratory of his?'

Eva blinked her pale blue eyes. 'I –'

'How can you work for that man? Why do you help him?' Bela wrenched her arm away and ran up the stairs to her room.

THE STINK OF GUILT

That evening, Bela didn't go down for dinner. She knew she wouldn't be able to swallow a single morsel sitting opposite her uncle and Dr Krol. Instead, she rang the bell and told the maid she was tired, that she'd have dinner in her room.

After she'd eaten, there was much to think about. She didn't waste any time on Dr Krol or the professor: she already knew exactly what she thought about them. It was Eva who was difficult to work out. The artefacts and preserving Bela's father's written work were all she seemed to care about. She looked like an angel with her halo of shining white hair, and Bela's father must have liked her. Even so, she could be a part of the deceit that Bela had tasted in the house. Something about her wasn't right.

Bela gazed at the photograph of her parents on the bedside table. If only they were here to love her, to show her what to do now. She picked up the journal she'd taken from her father's study. Perhaps she'd learn something about her parents in its pages.

There were endless lists of provisions and equipment for the upcoming expedition – how much animal feed, how many horses and dogs would be needed. Occasionally, there were descriptions and sketches of the tribespeople he had met living on the Siberian plains. Bela knew her mother had been a member of one of those nomadic tribes, and she hoped to find some mention of her. But there was none.

She turned back to the flyleaf. The date at the beginning of the journal was 1893, seventeen years ago, so perhaps it was before her parents had met. Eva had said her father kept detailed notes on all his expeditions and Bela wondered if there was a more recent journal. She would ask.

She opened the notebook again at random and found a sketch of the lion-headed man, along with a description of the cave in which it was found. It wasn't the only drawing of the mysterious artefact. Page after page was given over to detailed sketches and ideas about its possible meaning. Bela was arrested by one note in particular.

*The lion-headed man has taken over my
imagination. I cannot stop thinking about
him. He invades my every dream. I have
returned to the site where the figure
was found to excavate further and I have
enlisted the help of a local tribesman,
Arno.*

Arno? The driver who'd brought Bela to the estate?

She read on. There was a map of the site and
sketches of stone tools, showing where they'd been
found. There was also a drawing of Arno – Bela
recognized his narrow dark eyes. Underneath, her
father had written,

*I do not know how I ever managed
without him. He knows this whole area
well and persuades the most unfriendly
chiefs to show us where they have found
pieces of interest. We have a few words
of each other's languages now and I find
I like the man. He is good company and
fiercely loyal.*

Bela flicked ahead and found Arno's name mentioned

everywhere. He had obviously played an important part in her father's work.

An idea began to form in Bela's head. Was Arno with her father on his last expedition? Did he know something about his disappearance? Bela put the journal down on the bedside table. Tomorrow she would find him and ask him what he knew.

She blew out the candle and lay there for a long time, listening to the owls calling to each other in the woods. As she stared into the darkness, the picture that came to her mind was the rock crystal hanging round the professor's neck. It had seemed a strange thing for him to be wearing. She'd only glimpsed it for a second before her uncle tucked it away, but the luminous stone had seared its image into her mind and now she found she could recall every shimmering detail.

At last she slept, but the night was as confused and unsettling as the day had been. She dreamed the magpie sat outside her window, rapping on the glass with its black beak. *Wake up*, the bird's tapping seemed to say. *You're not safe here.*

When Bela suddenly came to, she found herself standing on the balcony wall outside her open window. She grabbed the edge of the roof to steady herself and climbed back in.

Her heart was still hammering as she got into

bed, but it wasn't the thought of falling that made her fearful. She knew at once what the professor and Dr Krol would make of the incident. They'd say she was mad, just like her mother.

The next morning, as Bela was dressing, she heard the carriage driving away. She rushed downstairs, bumping into Eva in the hall. 'Where's Arno gone?'

'He's taking Doctor Krol to town,' Eva replied.

'When will he be back?'

'This afternoon, I expect.' She gave Bela a curious look. 'Is there anything I can help you with?'

Bela was itching to ask Arno about her father's last expedition, but she did her best to sound unconcerned. 'No. Just wondering.'

It was mid-afternoon when Arno returned. He drew the horses up in front of the house, jumped down and opened the carriage door for Dr Krol. He was followed by two men in military greatcoats and caps, one with a filthy bandage covering his eye. They saluted the doctor before following him into the house.

Bela continued to watch as Arno led the horses away. She waited half an hour, went downstairs and slipped out through the back door.

The stables were tucked away behind the house, a narrow, single-storey brick building with a chimney and forge at one end. Arno was in the hay-strewn courtyard out the front, working with another man who was helping him change one of the horse's shoes.

Bela called out to him, but he didn't reply. For a moment, Bela was confused – did he mean to ignore her? But when he'd finished nailing the shoe, he waved the other man away, wiped his hands on his leather apron and came over.

'I wanted to talk to you about my father,' Bela said. 'You knew him, didn't you?'

Arno said nothing. He kept his eyes fixed on the stained rag he was clutching. Anyone else would have thought the man ignorant or rude, but Bela could tell, from the sour-milk taste that seeped from every pore, that Arno was afraid.

Dr Krol had claimed Arno didn't speak Polish or Russian, but the journal mentioned he and Bela's father had a few words of each other's languages. She tried again. 'I've been reading his journal.'

Arno stopped wiping his hands. She had his attention now and she could see, despite what Krol had said, that he understood her Polish perfectly well.

'He mentions you a lot,' she said. 'About how much you helped him, how loyal you were.'

He raised his head then and his dark gaze seemed to rest on Bela's face, although it felt as if he was looking right through her, at something far away in the mountains beyond.

'Were you with him on his final expedition?'

Arno gave no answer, but his fists tightened round the rag.

Bela's heartbeat quickened. 'You *were* there, weren't you?'

The driver put his hands up and began to back away. Bela gritted her teeth in frustration. Why was the man being so evasive?

'Arno, please, I know you understand me.'

He shook his head, turned abruptly and began to walk quickly towards the stables.

Bela ran alongside him. 'Why won't you talk to me? What are you trying to hide?' She grabbed his arm and pulled him round to face her. 'My father said you were a good man. He trusted you.' She hadn't meant to get upset, but now there were angry tears in her eyes. 'Maybe that was his mistake. Maybe you weren't worthy of his trust.'

Suddenly Eva appeared from the back of the house and came hurrying towards them. 'What's going on?'

'I'm trying to find out what happened to my father,' Bela said. 'But *he* won't tell me anything.'

'Leave him alone!' Eva put a protective arm round Arno's shoulders. 'Can't you see you're upsetting him?'

'What's he got to be upset about?' Bela snapped back. 'I'm the one who's lost both of my parents.'

Eva glanced up at the house, at the many windows that overlooked them. 'Go back inside before you get us all into trouble.'

Bela folded her arms. 'Not until Arno tells me what he knows.'

Eva looked towards the house again. 'We can't talk here.' She led them all round the back of the stables. As soon as they were hidden from view, she turned on Bela. 'You should never have come to Wilder House. It was bad for your father and for your mother and now it'll be bad for you too.'

She sounded angry, but Bela could taste her fear. 'All I want is some answers about my father's disappearance, but Arno pretends he can't understand me, although I know he does perfectly well.'

'Oh, he understands you all right.' Eva turned to Arno and patted his hand. 'But he'll never be able to tell you anything.'

'Why not?'

Arno had been staring at the ground, his shoulders hunched up by his ears. But now he raised his head and opened his mouth wide.

Bela drew back, horrified. Where Arno's tongue should have been, there was nothing. She turned away.

'Now do you see?' Eva put her arm back round Arno's shoulders and guided him into the stables.

Bela tried to follow, but Eva blocked the doorway.

'You're hiding something,' Bela said. 'Both of you. I know you are.'

'Why don't you mind your own business?' Eva said. 'Or, even better, go back to where you came from.' She seemed to realize she'd gone too far and lowered her voice. 'I'm only saying this for your own good. Go back to Kraków – you were much better off there.' She closed the door in Bela's face.

There was nothing for Bela to do but go back to the house. She climbed the stairs to her room and stood at the window, looking out across the treetops. The image of Arno's open mouth kept flashing into her mind.

Who had done that to him?

Then there was Eva. She was hiding something, and she wanted Bela gone, that much was clear. Yet among all the secretive flavours that swirled round her, Bela had not tasted one that showed Eva meant her any harm.

Bela turned away from the window and threw herself down on the bed. She was no nearer to finding out the truth about her father's last expedition. All she'd managed to do was create a whole new set of troubling questions. The only thing she could say for certain was that there was something between Eva and Arno, who were both infused with the same long-fermented flavour. They both stank of guilt.

The attic in the west wing

The cold woke Bela up. She'd been dreaming about the magpie tapping at her window, so she was not completely shocked to find herself outside again in the middle of the night. She struggled into a sitting position and felt around in the darkness. Behind her there was a brick wall. Beneath, a rough floor made of wooden planks, and, beyond it, nothing but open air. Out to the side, her searching fingers closed round a wooden pole. She realized she was up on the scaffolding that covered the west wing of the house. It seemed impossible, but somehow she must have got on to the roof and climbed across it while she slept.

The thought of being high above the ground in darkness terrified her, but she told herself not to panic.

There was a faint pink smudge in the sky. All she had to do was wait, shivering, until there was enough light to climb down.

Soon she could make out the grid of wooden poles. She peered over the edge and her stomach flipped; she was perched at the very top of the scaffolding.

Maybe she should wait. Someone would come out and see her eventually. Bela considered this for a moment, but the thought of her uncle and Dr Krol discovering she was a sleepwalker convinced her to try and get down by herself.

She shuffled to the end of the platform. Round the corner was a window on the same level. She crawled to it and peered in at a dim corridor on the other side. She pressed her fingers against the sash and pushed. To her relief, the window slid open. She swung a leg over the sill and climbed in.

The floor was thick with dust, but a pathway had been cleared by someone's footsteps. She followed the trail to a door and stood there for a moment, listening for any sound coming from the other side.

Silence.

She pushed the door open and shivered as a wave of freezing air rolled over her. The room was full of lumpen objects covered in sheets. She could see the outline of iron bedsteads, and her first thought was of furniture stored in the attic, only the taste inside the room told her a different story. The air in here was foetid, but it didn't have the damp, mushroomy flavour of abandonment she'd expected. It was dense and alive.

Just inside the door was a table with a steel syringe and what looked like medical equipment lying on top. Bela picked up a length of rubber tubing attached to an empty glass bottle that had an overwhelming metallic smell of blood.

All Bela wanted was to get away from that room, but she had to know what was going on in her uncle's house. With her pulse beating at the root of her tongue, she edged towards the nearest shrouded mound and lifted the corner of the sheet.

A man lay underneath.

She dropped the sheet and stifled a cry. For a moment, she just stood there, her hand pressed to her mouth. At first she thought the man was dead. But she could hear the faint sound of breathing and the vivid taste in the air told her he still clung to life. He must be fast asleep.

She lifted the sheet again. The man was dressed in a sealskin parka, the fur-lined hood pulled up over his head. Across his chest he held a rifle, like the ones she'd seen in the cabinet in the professor's study.

Her determination to understand was stronger than her fear, so she stretched out a hand and nudged the man's shoulder. He didn't stir. Why wouldn't he wake up? She nudged him again, harder this time, but he continued to lie still.

Bela glanced round the room and counted twenty-four of the shrouded shapes. She crept from one to another, lifting the corners of the sheets. A sleeping stranger, armed and dressed in sealskins, lay underneath each one.

Then she saw a face that seemed familiar. The man had a bandage across one eye. Wasn't he one of the soldiers she'd seen getting out of the carriage with Dr Krol?

Bela looked over at the window. Morning was not far away. Soon the house would be awake and she must not be found here in the forbidden wing of the house. She crept out of the room and to the end of the corridor, where a narrow spiral staircase led to the floor below.

Bela began to make her way down and, after a couple of turns, she saw a door ahead. But before she could reach it, she heard the scrape of a key in the lock. The door swung open and Eva came through. 'Oh!' she said, stopping dead when she saw Bela.

Bela was just as shocked. She stood frozen on the staircase, her heart thudding in her chest.

From behind Eva came Dr Krol's voice. 'Miss Balinsky? What is it?'

Eva said nothing, only blinked her pale eyes at Bela. It lasted no more than a moment, but in that brief time Bela saw a change come over Eva's face, as if she'd finally come to a difficult decision. She pressed her lips together and turned round, blocking the doorway. 'I've just realized, Doctor Krol, that I've left my shawl downstairs and it's very chilly in the attic.' She laughed girlishly. 'I don't suppose . . .'

Bela heard the doctor's irritated reply. 'Of course. I'd be delighted to fetch it for you.'

When he'd gone, Eva turned back to Bela. 'Quickly! He can't see you here.'

She took Bela's hand and pulled her through the doorway that emerged on the same floor as Bela's bedroom.

'How did you get up there?' she whispered. Before Bela could reply, she shook her head. 'It doesn't matter.

Go back to your room and don't say anything about this to anybody.' Eva went to leave, but Bela grabbed her hand. 'Who are those people up there?'

Eva glanced over her shoulder. 'He'll be back any minute.'

'What's going on in this house?'

Eva flapped her hands to quieten her. 'There's no time to explain now . . . Listen, I'll meet you at five o'clock, in the woods by the gates. I'll tell you everything then, I promise.'

Bela slipped back to her room. She climbed into bed, pulled the blankets up to her chin and rubbed her frozen limbs. It was a long time before her chasing heartbeat slowed and she was warm again. She lay in the half-light, eyes wide open. When she'd blundered into Eva on the stairs, she'd seen her surprise, the split-second decision that flashed across her face. Eva hadn't given her up, but was she a friend or an enemy? She obviously knew about the men in the attic. Bela's mind went back to the dim, shrouded bedsteads, the gun each sleeping man held across his chest. She couldn't make sense of it. They must be an experiment of the professor's, like the rat. But who were they and why wouldn't they wake up?

Eva

Just before five o'clock, Bela slipped out of the house. The day was overcast and cold, and the grass around the empty flower beds was petrified with frost. She could taste snow on the air, the approach of winter.

As she walked away from the house, she felt its looming presence behind her and glanced over her shoulder. The many windows stared back. She deliberately made her way along the path that led to the little graveyard in the woods. If anyone saw her, they'd think she was going to visit her mother.

She lost herself among the trees, and when she was sure she could no longer be seen, she changed direction and made for the gates. She was almost there when Eva stepped out from among the trees. She had a huge dog with her, who made a deep rumbling in its throat at Bela's approach.

'It's not safe here,' Eva said. 'Come.'

She led Bela away from the gates and didn't stop until they were deep in the woods. 'No one comes here, and if they do, Pavlov will warn us.' She nodded towards the dog, who stood apart like a sentinel, alert to the surrounding forest.

'I've got something for you.' Eva unbuttoned her coat and took out a slim, leather-bound book. 'Whatever you do, don't let your uncle or Krol know you have it.'

Bela turned to the flyleaf, where she read her father's name and the date, 1895, two years before she was born. 'So there *is* another journal! Where did you get it?'

'Arno has kept it hidden all these years.'

'Why?'

Eva sat down on the trunk of a fallen tree and motioned for Bela to join her. 'Read it and you'll see.'

Bela tucked the journal under her coat. For a moment, they sat in silence, and then Bela said, 'I asked you before, but you didn't give me a proper answer. Was my mother mad?'

Eva sighed. 'She was unlike anyone I've ever met, but no, she wasn't mad.'

'Then why was she locked up?'

'When your father disappeared, the family met to decide what to do. I'm sure you know how much your great-aunt disapproved of your parents' liaison and she was quick to accept Krol's diagnosis. The professor claimed the estate, and as you were so young it seemed to make sense for Olga to take you back to Kraków. Nagar was to stay here.'

'Didn't she want to come with me?'

Eva's face crumpled. 'She was given no choice. All that was needed was a doctor's signature to certify her madness.'

An image of Krol flashed into Bela's mind, a man so smooth he could slip through your fingers. 'Olga said my mother sent me away.'

'No,' Eva said. 'You were *taken* from her. She said you'd come back, that you would avenge her.'

Bela's breathing quickened. 'What did she mean by that?'

'I don't know. You were only a baby. It didn't seem to make much sense.'

'And you?' Bela said. 'What did you do while all this was going on?'

Eva turned her face away. 'What could I have done against Doctor Krol? I'm only a woman, little more than a servant. Who would listen to me?'

Bela squeezed her eyes shut. Everyone had abandoned her mother. Even, in a way, Bela herself, and she was uncomfortably aware of the taste of her own guilt. She'd taken her cue from the adults around her, but was that really any excuse? Not once had she asked to see her mother. Like everyone else, she'd been too ashamed to mention her. Bela felt a freezing pinprick on her cheek. She opened her eyes and looked up, past the treetops to the white sky above. A few flakes of snow twined slowly down through the cold air and she let them settle on her face.

'Maybe you couldn't help her,' she said at last, 'but that doesn't explain why you've been working for my

uncle all these years.'

Eva wrung her hands. 'He said he would continue Sacha's work. He said we'd further his research together.'

Bela remembered how Eva's face had glowed as she talked about her father's books, his artefacts. The professor was clever. He'd known how to reel her in.

The dog whined and trotted over. It laid its head across Eva's lap and she gently stroked its ears. 'He promised to keep your mother safe.'

'And you believed him?'

'When you read the journal, you'll understand. Your uncle said everyone would want a piece of her, that she'd be torn apart if anyone found out where she came from.'

A shiver of dread ran through Bela's body. 'What do you mean? Where *did* she come from?'

Eva stood. 'I have to go.'

'But I still don't understand –'

'Read the journal – it will explain everything. Be

ready to leave first thing in the morning.' She caught Bela's eye. 'You must be gone before the professor returns.'

She turned to go, but Bela caught her hand. 'Am I really in danger?'

Eva nodded once. 'Doctor Krol will sign a paper to certify your madness and then you'll never be able to leave.'

THE LOST JOURNAL

That evening, as soon as dinner was over, Bela rushed up to her room. She locked herself in and took out the journal. She held it close to her face, hoping for some lingering flavour of her father, but all she could taste was the dust that clung to the binding.

She opened the notebook and began to read. Again, there were lists and preparations for the forthcoming expedition, but the notes in between showed how excited her father had been. He was planning to return to the glacier where he'd found the lion-headed man. *The find of the century*, he called it, real proof at last that the ancestors of modern humans were not ignorant brutes. He said the figure proved they were artists, people with strong spiritual beliefs.

Bela soon found the notes her father had written on the expedition.

1 SEPTEMBER 1895
We staked out an area to excavate where there were layers of ice that fell as snow twenty, thirty, even forty thousand years ago. In the afternoon, we uncovered many stone tools. They're not like the ones made by Homo sapiens or the ones attributed to Neanderthals either. I wonder if we have discovered the tools of an entirely separate human species.

On the next page, it looked as though the note had been written in haste or with a shaking hand.

2 SEPTEMBER 1895
Today we made an astonishing find. A human body in its entirety, lying face down.

4 SEPTEMBER 1895
We have been digging for two days. We have chipped the ice away and her body

— we can see it's a woman now — is almost completely exposed. Her hair, her fingernails, even the eagle feathers of her cloak. Everything is perfectly preserved.

5 SEPTEMBER 1895

It is now two o'clock in the morning and I cannot sleep. It is with some uncertainty that I record the strange things that happened yesterday. We spent the daylight hours digging, but when evening came I was unwilling to return to the camp with the others and I stayed behind.

When darkness fell, I lit a hurricane lamp and held it close to the ice-woman's face. There was a string of leather hanging from her lips that seemed attached to something inside her mouth. I stood for a long time, wondering at the preservation of her skin, and as I looked into that face, which was ancient and yet still young, I thought I saw one eyelid blink. I am ashamed to say I was so overwhelmed by fear that I dropped the lamp and ran all the way back to the camp.

*I can only think I'm overtired. I
haven't slept properly for several nights
and I let my imagination run away with
me. What tricks the mind plays on us!*

Bela could feel the uneasy excitement in her father's
words. It was almost as if he was speaking directly
to her. She glanced over at the photograph of her
parents, her father's protective hand on her mother's
belly. How she wished she'd known him. If her father
had lived, she would have had a place in the world, a
family. She would have belonged.

By now it was late, and she got undressed and
climbed into bed. Although she was tired, Bela turned
back to the journal. Up until then, her father had given
an almost daily account, but as she flicked ahead she
saw the next few pages spanned several years.

20 DECEMBER 1895
*I hardly know how to begin. We returned
to Wilder House three months ago, but
it is only now I feel I understand enough
to write about what happened. I should
start with that extraordinary night. After
writing in my journal about the strange
things I'd seen, I returned to my bed,*

*but sleep would not come. I got up, took a
lamp and went out to the glacier. To my
horror, I found the body gone and only
a void in the ice where it had been. I
looked about me in the darkness and saw
a figure standing close by. It defied all
logic, but I knew at once that it was her,
the woman I had found in the ice.*

Bela's heart thudded in her chest. It had to be a mistake.
How could anyone come alive after all those years? She
turned back to the journal, all tiredness gone, but the
next entry in the journal was written months later.

*10 FEBRUARY 1896
I wonder if I have done the right thing
in bringing her here. She cannot settle
and constantly looks about her at the
strangeness of everything she sees. I have
decided to write to my brother Viktor
and ask him to come. As a psychologist,
he may have some useful insights. I dare
not look outside the family for help. I fear
to expose her to the outside world – she
would become a curiosity if anyone were
to see her extraordinary black eyes.*

Bela snapped the notebook shut. She remembered the dream on the train, the woman with a face like hers whose eyes were entirely black. Her heart thudded in her chest as she remembered what Eva had said – that her mother would have been torn apart if anyone found out where she came from.

Bela took the candle, went over to the mirror and peered at her reflection in the dim light. She opened her eyes wide. They looked normal, just like anyone else's. Yet suddenly she knew in her heart, more than ever before, that she wasn't like anyone else. She gazed at the triangle of dots tattooed on her palm. The meaning of all this was pressing at the edges of her mind, but it felt too vast, too overwhelming.

Bela returned to bed and read on. She was not surprised when, a page later, Bela's father reported the name of the woman: Nagar. As the journal said, it defied all logic, but the woman he'd found buried in the ice was Bela's mother. A mother who was many thousands of years old, a mother who was a different species of human altogether.

After that, the journal detailed her parents' growing liking for each other. This soon turned to love and Bela's tears fell on to the pages as she read of their plan to marry. There was even a description of the wedding ceremony. As Eva had said, it was not a Christian service but a ritual of Nagar's people. They each cut a long wound in the palm of their hand and clasped them together to exchange their blood, to become one.

On the next page she found the news of her own birth. There was only the date, 7 May 1897, and a single line,

We have a beautiful daughter.

Here it was: proof that she had once been loved. She had to stop reading as fresh tears poured down her cheeks.

There were no further notes until the spring of 1898, when preparations began for what Bela knew would be her father's final expedition.

I have learned much from my wife about the place she has been living in. Usta, the totem she wears about her neck, contains an ancient world that mirrors the geography of our own, but made of spirit rather than physical matter. I can hardly contain my excitement. The thought that I will soon see all this for myself is beyond the dreams of any scientist.

Following this were the usual meticulous lists of provisions and plans. Bela was horrified to see her uncle's name mentioned many times in glowing terms. It seemed Arno and Viktor would accompany her father on the expedition and watch over him while he entered Nagar's spirit world.

With a sinking heart, she read on. Here, there was a sketch of an orb-shaped stone strung on a length of rawhide, which Bela recognized immediately. It was the luminous crystal she had seen hanging round the professor's neck.

Underneath the sketch, Bela's father had written:

All I need to do is place the totem under my tongue and it will carry me to the spirit world of my wife's people. Only those who carry the blood of Nagar's clan are admitted, but, since our marriage, her blood runs in my veins and she has assured me that the spirits who guard the entrance will give way.

Reading this was torture for Bela. She was hurtling towards the end of the journal, unable to prevent the disaster she knew was coming.

It was late into the night when she finished the last few entries. They recorded her father's plan to put himself to sleep in the snow, as Nagar and her people had done all those thousands of years ago.

And then, tired out, Bela drifted off to sleep, and the writing and her dream merged into one continuous story. She saw what must have happened as if she was actually there – the professor creeping up to her father's sleeping body, wrenching the totem from his mouth and leaving him in the snow for dead.

THE TOTEM

There was a flutter of wings, the feeling of feathers against her skin and Bela woke with a start. The horror of the dream stayed with her, skulking among the shadows in the corners of her room. Could it really be true, or was it just a dream? Bela remembered the photograph in her father's study, her uncle's narrowed eyes as he loomed over his little brother. He must have always hated him. But why? Could he have loathed him so much that he *murdered* him?

It was hard to believe that anyone could do such a terrible thing, but the totem proved what she'd dreamed was true. The professor must have taken it from her father, so that he could travel to the spirit world. Only one other person knew what really happened. Arno. And he would never be able to tell anyone the truth.

Bitter rage raced through Bela's blood. Before, her father had only been a shadowy idea in her mind, nothing more than a dream. Now she felt she understood him; his journal had brought him to life and, at the same time, revealed the way in which he had been taken from her.

She got out of bed and went over to the window. It was still hours until dawn and the stars blazed in the cloudless sky. Eva was right. Bela was in grave danger. The journal had laid it all bare: her uncle had used her mother's blood to cross into the spirit world himself, and he must have taken all those people with him – all the sleeping bodies in the west wing. She remembered the syringe, the bottle and the rubber tubing she'd found in the attic that must have been used to transfuse the blood.

If Bela didn't leave now, the professor would lock her up and use her blood to take more men to the spirit world.

Her mind went back and forth over what was best to do. She could leave today, with Arno, but then she would never know the whole truth. She would never see the world of her mother's ancestors.

My ancestors, she said to herself.

The thought of being at her uncle's mercy horrified her. But she could not give up the chance to discover who she was, to find a place where she truly belonged. Hadn't she always said she was no one's sacrifice?

At last she came to a decision. She would not wait helplessly for the professor's vile plan to play out. In Bela's mind, another plan was forming.

An hour later, there was a quiet knocking and Eva slipped in. 'Arno will have the carriage ready soon.' She glanced round the room. 'Where are your bags? Haven't you packed?'

'I'm not leaving.'

'But you must! Haven't you read the journal?'

'I've read it. I know what happened . . . I know my mother was from another time.'

Eva put a hand on Bela's arm. 'It must be a shock.'

'I don't think I've really understood it all yet . . . I feel there's so much more to know, to find out.'

Eva smiled sadly. 'That's just the sort of thing your father would've said.'

Bela turned to her. 'I've learned so much about him from the journal and I feel I must find out what happened to him. But listen, I know the professor was taking my mother's blood. Is that why she died? Is that what killed her?'

Eva bit her lip. 'I don't know for sure. As I told you, I hadn't seen her for years and it would be impossible to prove. But I've racked my brains, and what other explanation is there?'

Bela went to the window, not wanting Eva to see her furious tears. She dashed them away and gazed out at the world beyond the glass. The moon had gone down long ago and the silent forest lay in darkness. She remembered what Eva had said: her mother believed that Bela would avenge her, and she promised herself that one day she would make her uncle pay for what he'd done.

'What do you know of the professor's plan?' she said to Eva.

'Not much. But the men in the attic are mercenaries. He's taken an army into the other world.'

Bela thought for a moment. 'Where does he take himself when he goes there? Do you know?'

Eva nodded. 'He goes to his quarters on the other side of the house, beyond his study.'

'Does anyone go in there while he's asleep?'

'No. He keeps the door locked.' Eva looked at her fearfully. 'What are you planning to do?'

'Do you have a key?'

'No.'

'Does anyone?'

'Only the professor.'

Bela thought for a moment. 'Tell Arno I will need his help tomorrow.'

'But the professor will be awake again by then. It'll be too late! He won't let you leave.'

'Tell Arno I won't be going to the train station.'

'Then where?' Eva frowned. 'What are you planning to do?'

'I'm going to take the totem away from the professor, just like he took it from my father.'

'And then what?'

Bela went to the window and looked out across the dark forest. 'I will find the place my father tried to reach. I'll go to the spirit world of my mother's people.'

That night, as soon as the house was quiet, Bela got dressed in her warmest clothes. She pulled on a pair of jodhpurs – a skirt was no good for what she intended. Her boots she left off. During the day, the sky had clouded over and snow had come down heavily. It was freezing outside and the smooth soles would slip, so she'd be better off without them. Earlier, Bela had sneaked into the kitchens and taken a small paring knife, which she now slipped into her pocket.

She went to the window, slid it open and stuck her head out. A bright moon lit the snowy ground, four floors beneath her. If she had managed to get on to the roof and climb across to the other side of the house fast asleep, surely she could do it now, wide awake? The long drop below the balcony made her heart race, but a locked door hadn't kept her out last time and it wouldn't now.

She climbed on to the parapet. It was covered in thick snow and her bare feet burned with the cold. She gripped the edge of the eaves and pulled herself up. Her legs scrabbled at the empty air, but she got a foothold on one of the stone gargoyles framing the window and heave herself on to the roof.

She crawled up the sloping tiles, but they were slippery with snow and she began to slide back towards the edge. She managed to stop herself by lying spread-eagled on the tiles and pushing herself up an inch at a time, trying to ignore the cold that seeped through her clothes and bled into her body and her bones.

Finally her aching fingers closed round the curved tiles that lay along the apex of the roof. Beside her was the solid brick of a chimney stack and she grabbed

on to it and pulled herself up the rest of the way. Ahead of her, she could see the blunt ends of the scaffolding poles sticking up at the edge of the roof. It looked a long way away.

She put both hands on the ridge tiles and, gripping the slope on either side with her knees, shifted along the roof. *Don't think about falling*, she told herself, and *don't look down.*

Eventually she reached the end of the roof and peered cautiously over the edge. There was a platform of wooden planks suspended on the scaffolding beneath her. If she could drop down to it, she'd be able to reach the ladders that had been lashed into the grid and get to the floors below. It sounded easy, but up here, four storeys high, it was a different matter.

She grabbed hold of the nearest pole. In her mind's eye, she saw herself wrenched away by gravity, falling into empty space, but she gritted her teeth, twisted her legs round the pole and slid to the platform below. From there, she climbed down the ladders to the first floor and skirted round the front of the house.

At last she stood in front of the window that led to the professor's quarters. For a moment, Bela closed her eyes and took several deep breaths, steeling herself against what might lie ahead. Then she braced her fingers under the wood of the sash and pushed. But her frozen fingers were weak and the window was stuck tight. She was glad she'd brought the knife, and she worked the point of the blade under the frame and pressed down hard on the handle. The window gave way and the casement shifted open with a loud crack.

Bela froze, imagining her uncle waking, coming to the window and finding her. But the night remained silent and Bela remembered the men in the attic. She reminded herself this was no ordinary sleep, that the professor would not be woken by any amount of noise.

Bela stepped over the sill into the freezing gloom of her uncle's room. A solitary gas lamp burned above a four-poster bed in which a figure lay, shrouded in a sheet. She crept across the room, screwed up her courage and drew back the sheet.

As she gazed down at her uncle's grey, slumbering face, she thought about what he had done to her parents. A hot wave of anger swept through her body and her fingers tightened round the handle of the knife.

For a few seconds, Bela didn't know what she would do, but as suddenly as it had come, her anger waned. *I'm not like him*, she thought.

She put the knife back in her pocket. She'd come for the shining stone and she could see its leather strap hanging from his mouth. All she had to do was take it. Holding her breath, she took hold of the strap and gave it a sharp tug. The professor's mouth fell open and the totem slid out.

Terrified the professor would wake without the totem, she went straight to the door, unlocked it and went through to her uncle's study before locking it again from the other side.

Now she took a moment to examine the shining stone. It tasted of earth and tarnished metal, like the lion-headed figure she'd seen in her father's study. Only there was nothing subtle about its flavour, and the taste of ancient power burned like fire on her tongue. She tied the strap round her neck and the totem hung at her throat, heavy and reassuring, as if it had found the place it wanted to be.

It had belonged to her mother. Now it was hers.

When Bela emerged from the professor's quarters, she found Eva pacing up and down in the corridor. 'Did you get it?'

Bela nodded.

Eva let out a sigh of relief. 'Quickly then. Arno is ready and the house will soon be stirring.'

Eva turned to go, but Bela held her back. 'Do you think the professor will wake now I have the totem?'

Eva shook her head. 'It was the totem and your mother's blood that allowed him to go back and forth between the worlds. Now he'll remain in the spirit world, just like all those men sleeping in the attic.'

Eva led the way down to the hall and through the kitchen to the back door. 'Change into these.' She handed Bela a parka, leggings, gloves and a pair of boots, all made of sealskin.

When Bela was dressed, she turned to Eva. 'Thank you for everything.'

Eva smiled sadly. 'I only hope it makes up, just a little, for the things I should've done before.'

They hugged each other tightly. 'Take care,' Eva said. 'I'll stay here and wait for your return.'

Bela went out of the house and ran towards the stables, where Arno was waiting for her.

'Look,' she said, holding the totem up. 'I've taken it back from him.'

The crystal twisted backwards and forwards on its leather strap. In its soft light, Bela saw a smile curl at the corner of Arno's lips, the first she'd seen on his face.

He heaved a rucksack on to his shoulders and they set off. There was no point asking him where they were going since Arno could not reply. But Bela knew it would be many miles from the house, a place where, like her father before her, she would lie down in the snow, put the totem under her tongue and fall asleep.

PART TWO

THE SPIRIT WORLD

HOW THE SPIRIT WORLD
CAME TO BE

In the beginning, there was only one world. Everyone had to share it, both the living and the dead. But as time went on, the dead came to outnumber the living. The dead were silent hunters and they trapped all the game and ate all the elk, all the reindeer and the snow hares, leaving nothing for those who were alive. The living starved and added to the multitude of those who were dead.

The guardian spirits, Eagle, Raven and Crow, went to the Mother-of-All to ask what could be done. As they approached her lair, they found the remains of many creatures piled up outside. The spirits knew Mother did not like to be disturbed while she was eating, but the situation was urgent, so they gathered their courage and drew close to the mouth of the cave.

'Help us, Mother-of-All!' the spirits cried. 'Or the People who are still living will die.'

A loud burp came from inside the cave. 'Come back later,' Mother said. 'I have just eaten a big meal and I need to rest.'

'What shall we do?' Crow said. 'It will take many years for Mother to sleep off such an enormous feast, by which time all the People will be dead.'

'We could go inside the cave and beg for help,' Raven said. 'But it is well known that Mother gobbles up any creature that annoys her.'

Eagle looked around at the piles of bones. Every single one had been picked clean of meat and sinew and fat. 'Do not be afraid, sisters,' Eagle said. 'Mother is so full up she will not have room to swallow the three of us.'

So the spirits entered the cave and crept up to Mother's nest.

'What do you want now?' Mother said. 'I was about to sleep.' And she opened her beak wide and yawned.

The three spirits peered inside Mother's gaping maw. They could see down her throat and into her stomach. There they beheld a shining moon and stars, like frozen drops of dew, twinkling in the darkness of the night sky.

'There is a whole new world in Mother's belly,' Raven said.

'Exactly what we need,' Crow replied. 'But how shall we get her to give it up?'

'I have an idea,' Eagle said. 'Let us behave as we did when we were tiny chicks, demanding to be fed.'

So, despite the danger, the three sisters approached Mother's nest, where they squawked and fluttered their wings and pecked at her beak. The Mother-of-All is a fearsome creature, but no parent can refuse to feed their children, and at last she was forced to regurgitate the contents of her belly. She coughed up a shining stone, inside which an entire world was coiled.

This is how the spirit world was born. It was called Usta, which means to gulp down or swallow whole. In this way, the spirits gave the ancestors a home and the lives of their descendants were saved.

THE BIRD THAT PASSES
BETWEEN THE WORLDS

R en-*ya* lifted her face to the breeze and drew in a deep breath over her tongue. The deer she was stalking were close.

She had followed the tracks since dawn, two sets of deep-dipped prints in the snow. Now they took her across a frozen river valley and up a steep, treeless incline. The trail disappeared halfway up the storm-blasted rocks and appeared again where the wind had blown the snow into thick mounds.

At the top of the ridge, Ren-*ya* found them among the trees. The doe was up on her hind legs, her forelegs braced against the trunk of a pine tree as she stripped the bark with her teeth. Her faun stood mute and nervous behind.

Ren-*ya* kneeled and shrugged her backpack off. Never once taking her eyes from the deer, she drew an arrow from the quiver and fitted it to the gut string. She raised the bow, pulled the string back to her shoulder and took aim.

The doe jumped down from the tree and chewed the bark. The faun nosed her belly and she let him feed. She stood alert, eyes wide, her ears twitching this way and that.

Ren-*ya*'s breath stilled, clouded in the freezing air. Tension flowed out of her body and into the weapon. When she and the bow were as one, she let the string slip from her fingers. As Ren-*ya*'s arrow flew, some thin thread of scent or faraway sound spooked the doe and she leaped away into the forest.

Ren-*ya* scrambled up and ran to the fallen body of the faun. The stone tip of the arrow had pierced its heart and she watched its blood, a sudden red flower in the snow. It was better to take the baby than the mother. He'd die anyway without her.

She tore a feather from her hair and, laying it on the ground, bowed her head. 'I am Ren-*ya*, a living spirit, and I call on Eagle, Raven and Crow. I thank the guardians for this kill.'

Ren-*ya* threw a rope of twisted sinew over the branch of a tree, slipped a noose knot round the delicate pointed hoof of the faun's hind leg. She hauled it up and tied off the other leg so that it hung head down. The sinew creaked as the carcass swung, scattering blood in a figure of eight in the snow.

She opened her backpack and laid two stone tools on the ground. One was fine and thin, lashed to a smooth bone handle, perfect for cutting meat from bone. She picked up the knife and weighed it in her hand. Ren-*ya*'s mother had given it to her and, whenever she held it, she was reminded of her first kill. Ren-*ya* had only been a child back then and she'd stood over the body, shaking, the stone blade gripped in her hand. Tears had pooled in her eyes at the enormity of what she'd done.

Her mother had put her arm round her shoulder. 'Do not cry, Ren-*ya*. It was a clean kill and without death we cannot live.' It was a hard lesson to learn, but Ren-*ya* had since mastered the patient sequence of killing. Still, there was always some sadness in it.

As she began to butcher the carcass, a flurry of wings made her look up. It was a magpie landing on a snow-heavy branch overhanging the kill.

'Good timing,' she said to the bird.

She cut a fresh strip of liver and held her gloved fist up like a falconer. The magpie opened its wings and leaped to her hand, where it tore at the meat.

Ren-*ya* had found the bird not long after her

mother disappeared. He had been lying in the snow, half dead, a fledgling fallen from the nest. In a world where messages were always brought by birds, finding him had a meaning. Ren-*ya* had pulled off her balaclava and carefully wrapped him up. She took the bird home and nursed him back to health. Nothing was too much trouble. She fed him the best meat cut into tiny cubes. They sat in front of the fire together, the bird perched on her shoulder. She stroked his silky black feathers, which were not really black at all, but blue-green and iridescent like a butterfly's wing.

As the bird thrived and grew, Ren-*ya*'s deep sadness lifted. After many moons, she accepted the message the magpie had brought. She stopped wondering when her mother would be coming back because she knew she never would.

Now Ren-*ya* stroked the bird's feathers. 'I haven't seen you for a long time,' she said. 'Where have you been?' The bird leaned into her, rubbing its glossy head against her hand before returning to its meal. When it had finished, it hopped into the branches and kept watch over the kill.

Ren-*ya* went back to skinning the animal. Starting at the knee joints, she slid her blade between the hide and the white of the fat, careful to keep the fur from spoiling the meat. She quartered the carcass, rolled the hide and strapped it all to the small, light sledge she had carried on her back.

Ren-*ya* turned towards home. The morning had been foggy and the white-out had made her job easier, masking her scent and deadening the crunch and champ of her footsteps in the snow. Now the fog had cleared and the light was good. She squinted, lifting a hand to shield her eyes. From the high ground of the ridge, she could see for miles. All around, mountains reared up above the forest and climbed to snowy heights. One stood above the others, three ragged, lofty peaks split by ice and broken by the endless work of the wind. The lower slopes were cloaked in pine trees and the forest flowed like a river of dark lava, all the way from the foothills to the frozen sea.

Dragging the sledge behind her, Ren-*ya* set off. The bird flew ahead, taking the familiar path that led back home. But when they were within an hour's trek of her camp, the bird changed direction, signalling to Ren-*ya* with its tail.

The magpie always knew which way to go. Once, Ren-*ya* had lost her *smoke*, an ash-filled pouch that held the stories of the ancestors. She would never have found it if the bird hadn't helped her. In that vast wilderness, it was like trying to find a pebble on a mountain.

But the magpie had led her to the pine tree where the pouch was snagged on a twig by its broken strap. The *smoke* was Ren-*ya*'s most precious possession. Without it, she would never complete the *long winter* and she would never grow up.

Ren-*ya* had reached her twelfth year when the Last were still living in the waking world. As custom decreed, she had stood before the whole tribe, waiting to see which spirit would choose her as their own. In her heart, Ren-*ya* knew she was meant for Raven, and when the black-feathered bird flew to her shoulder and claimed her as a warrior, she was filled with joy. She had been preparing herself for this path all her life, but for the next year her training intensified. Malor, a great warrior, had been named as her teacher. He showed her how to fight, how to survive alone in the great forests, ready for the ordeal of the *long winter*. They made a good team: Ren-*ya* learned quickly, and no one knew the craft of combat and survival as well as Malor.

And then the Last put themselves to sleep in the ice and came to the spirit world. By then, Ren-*ya* was thirteen, the time when every child must come of age and begin their ordeal. As the cold of their first winter in the spirit world set in, she said goodbye to her mother, thanked her teacher and went to live in the forest, where she built a shelter and hunted for food all alone. Three moons later, when the sun hardly skimmed the horizon and the days were as dark as night, she returned to her people. She had survived the *long winter* alone. She had proved she was ready to come of age.

The day after she returned, her people prepared for Ren-*ya*'s renaming ceremony. The fire was lit and a pinch of *smoke* filled the surrounding forest with a purplish haze. Hebera summoned the spirits to witness a child grown, but the branches of the trees remained empty. The spirits did not come.

The next winter, Ren-*ya* returned to the forest and began the ordeal all over again. But the outcome was the same. Day turned to night and the year moved through the seasons, yet none among the Last grew older and they began to realize they never would. Time seemed to pass, yet the Last remained the same age as their bodies, which lay frozen and unchanging, deep within the icy glaciers of the world they'd left so many years before.

Ren-*ya* lived through the *long winter* countless times, but at the end of it all, she was still only thirteen years old. A child.

'You must be patient,' Ren-*ya*'s mother used to say. 'One day we will return to the waking world and you will grow up.'

'When will that be?'

Ren-*ya*'s mother shook her head. 'Who knows? You must keep hope anchored in your heart.'

She tried, but each time hope was torn away it took a piece of flesh with it, and now, when the year came to its end, Ren-*ya* no longer returned to her village. She stayed in the forest alone. It felt shameful to live among her people and remain a child.

The only medicine for despair was the *smoke*. When Ren-*ya* was at her lowest ebb, she would take a pinch of ash from her pouch and throw it in the fire. She would fall asleep and dream of the bravery of the ancestors, their patience and their hope. The stories she needed came to her and healed her – that was the magic of the *smoke* – and when she woke, her spirit was restored.

So now Ren-*ya* followed the magpie, although the way it took her would make her journey longer.

She was still an hour from the camp when the wind suddenly dropped and she breathed in a taste on the still air. The seam of flavour that came to her had some of the musk of her people, but it was mixed with something else, something she'd tasted before. The sharp, willow-sap flavour of the *white-eye*.

The mark of the Last

Ren-*ya* knew the *white-eyes* had invaded the spirit world of the Last, that somehow they'd managed to find a way in. She'd never seen them here in the spirit world herself, but sometimes she caught a hint of their flavour on the stiff breezes that blew across the ice. Some of her people had returned from the Big Forest with stories of sightings. Others who ventured there had disappeared and no one crossed the glacier or went as far as the Big Forest now.

Ren-*ya* left the sledge and went on cautiously, following the taste-trail to its source, an arrow ready on her bow.

Beneath the canopy of some close-growing pines she caught sight of the thing. A mounded shape in the half-light. She hunched down silently in the snow and watched it through the afternoon, but it didn't move once.

Was it dead? She stole closer, tasted the air. No, it was living but weakened. She crept up. Pointing her arrow where she judged its head to be, she nudged it with her foot, but it remained motionless.

She got down on her knees and rolled it over. Most of its face was hidden, wrapped in furs. She pulled one of its eyelids open. The dark-brown iris was small and round. It looked like a stone dropped into milk. She shuddered and pulled her hand away. Slowly, the lid closed itself again.

Ren-*ya* sat back on her heels. Was it a *white-eye*? It looked like one, but it tasted like something else. She would have questioned it if she could, made it tell her if there were others nearby. But the creature was well past speaking. She should just leave it where she found it. The thing was no threat and would die by itself before dark from the smell of it.

Ren-*ya* got up to go, dusting the snow from her clothing, but a chattering above her head made her glance up. The magpie was perched at the top of a larch, looking down at her.

'What?' she said.

At the sound of her voice, the magpie cocked its

head to one side.

'It is nothing to do with you,' Ren-*ya* said.

The bird tilted its head the other way.

Ren-*ya* clapped her hands at the magpie. 'Go on! Off you go!' But he didn't move.

She folded her arms across her chest. 'Stop looking at me like that. You are not my conscience, you know.'

The bird's unblinking black eye remained fixed on Ren-*ya*.

She sighed. 'All right then.'

She crouched down again. The thing was dressed in sealskins. No wonder it was half frozen; only a double layer of caribou was enough to keep out the cold at this time of year. She peered into its face. Truth is, it wasn't a *thing*. It was a person, a girl, and with her eyes closed she looked quite human. The bird was right: she couldn't leave her here. It wasn't far to Ren-*ya*'s camp and she might be able to revive her in front of the fire.

A voice buzzed in her head: *Think what the* white-eyes *have done to us.*

She took a piece of toughened sinew out of her pocket and tied the creature's hands and feet tightly together. There. She would take it back to the camp and save its life, but only so she could question it and find out what this *white-eye* knew.

Even with the sledge, it took more than an hour to

haul her back to the camp. By then, the girl's breathing was faint and shallow. She would die if she didn't get warmed soon.

Ren-*ya* dragged her into the shelter, but the fire had burned itself out. She took the birch-bark container she carried from her shoulder. Inside was a lump of slow-smouldering fungus wrapped in leaves. She used it to coax a flame from a small pile of pine needles and, when she had a good blaze going, she untied the girl's feet, pulled off her boots and rubbed at her skin with a piece of soft hide to get the blood flowing.

When some warmth had returned, Ren-*ya* tucked an elk's hide round her, then pulled back the hood and furs that hid the girl's face. It was then that she noticed the length of leather that was hanging from between the girl's teeth.

She pulled at the leather and an orb of white crystal slid from the girl's cracked lips and fell heavily into Ren-*ya*'s hand, where it lay, pulsing with glittering points of light.

For a long moment, all she could do was stare.

The totem had been worn by Ren-*ya*'s mother, but it belonged to all her people. It held the prophecy the ancestors had made. It was the doorway through which the spirits of the Last would one day return to their bodies, frozen in the ice of the waking world.

It was such a long time since her spirit had spoken to her body, and she trembled as she closed her hand tightly round the shining stone. At once, her mouth was flooded with the flavour of the waking world, the taste of ice and snow. She didn't notice time passing as she sat drawing strength from the whispered voices of the Last that filled the shelter.

When the whispering faded, she reluctantly tied the strap around the girl's neck and tucked the totem inside her tunic. Had the *white-eye* stolen it? Or had Ren-*ya*'s mother given it to her? She didn't know, but finding the girl in the snow was certainly no mistake. The magpie had led her there.

Night came on, but Ren-*ya* could not sleep. Each time she closed her eyes, the questions sprang up in her mind like a dense forest. In the quiet of the shelter, Ren-*ya* could hear the girl breathing, regular and strong. She would live, but then what? Why had she come? What did she want?

Ren-*ya* gave up trying to sleep. She got the hide pouch out of her backpack, took a precious pinch of the *smoke* and threw it on the fire. 'What should I do?' she asked. 'Should I take the totem from this girl?' A blue flame rose from the embers. There was a sound like someone drawing in their breath and the shelter filled with a haze of smoke. Ren-*ya* sank back on a pile of animal hides and breathed it in.

When she opened her eyes again, the story she'd been told was already drifting from her memory, but its message stayed with her.

The totem is not yours to take.

The girl woke in the night. She mumbled something and began to retch.

Ren-*ya* fetched a bowl and stuck it under the girl's chin. She spat into it and looked up. Her eyes widened, accentuating their white rims. She turned back to the bowl and heaved again, but this time nothing came up. She cleared her throat. 'I'm thirsty.'

Ren-*ya* fetched the water carrier and held it to her lips. 'Slowly,' she said when the girl gulped at it.

As she drank, Ren-*ya* watched. Reddish brown hair, the same colour as her own, lay in tangled strands across her shoulders.

'Enough,' Ren-*ya* said, snatching the water bottle away, 'or you will be sick again.'

The girl was trying to focus her eyes on Ren-*ya*'s

face. 'Who are you?' she managed to slur out.

'I am Ren-*ya*.'

The girl blinked at her. 'You speak a strange language . . . but I understand you.'

Ren-*ya* nodded. 'Spirit speaks to spirit . . .' But before she could finish her explanation, the girl's weird eyes slid shut and she fell back into unconsciousness.

It was early morning when Ren-*ya* was woken by a sharp kick. She sat up to find the girl glaring at her. 'Untie me!' she demanded.

Ren-*ya* rubbed her shoulder. 'Why would I do that?'

'I need to *go*!' The girl pressed her hands to her bladder.

Ren-*ya* took out her knife. 'If you try anything –' She made a stabbing movement with the blade to show what she would do. 'Understand?'

The girl nodded and got unsteadily to her feet.

'Put your boots on,' Ren-*ya* said.

'How? My hands are tied.'

Ren-*ya* licked her lips, tasted the air. This one had no weapons. She was thin and puny, too weak to be a real threat, but everyone knew the *white-eyes* were as sly as wolves. 'You can manage,' she said.

When she had pulled on her boots, Ren-*ya* shoved her out of the shelter. The girl gave her an evil look and staggered off behind the nearest trees.

Ren-*ya* nocked an arrow. 'Do not try to run,' she shouted after her, 'or I will shoot!'

'Run?' came the girl's voice. 'Out here?' She emerged from the trees, jumping from one foot to the other as she tugged her sealskin leggings back on. 'I mean –' she looked around – 'where would I go?'

'Back to the other *white-eyes* where you came from.'

'*White-eyes*? You mean . . . other people like me?' The girl frowned. 'Are they here? Have you seen them?'

Ren-*ya*'s arrow was already trained on the girl, but now she pulled the bowstring back to her shoulder. 'Do not pretend that you do not know.'

The girl didn't flinch, only narrowed her strange, white-rimmed eyes. 'I'm not one of *them*, if that's what you think.'

'What else could you be?' Ren-*ya* said.

'My name's Bela.' She smiled uncertainly. 'I'm not with those others . . . I don't mean you any harm.' As she spoke, the girl's hands went to her throat and curled absent-mindedly round the totem that dangled from her neck.

'Where did you get that?' Ren-*ya* said.

The girl glanced down at the crystal. 'I took it,' she said defiantly.

In one swift movement, Ren-*ya* stepped forward, grabbed the totem and wrenched it off. 'I knew you were a thief!'

The girl's nostrils flared. 'I didn't steal it!' She stared back, breathing hard.

Ren-*ya* sucked the air in through her teeth. The *white-eye* was not to be trusted. She wasn't *lying* exactly, but it didn't taste as if she was telling the whole truth. She put the totem in her pocket and jerked her head towards the shelter. 'Get back inside.'

The girl looked as if she was going to refuse, but her gaze came to rest on the bow in Ren-*ya*'s fist. She huffed in annoyance, lifted the flap of skin that covered the doorway and crawled in.

Ren-*ya* followed. 'Hold out your hands,' she said, checking the sinew was tied tightly round the girl's wrists.

'At least let me warm them a bit; they're freezing cold.' The girl tugged off her gloves with her teeth and held her hands out to the smouldering embers of the fire.

Ren-*ya* gasped.

It couldn't be. The girl had a tattoo on her hand, a series of dots making a three-sided shape. For Ren-*ya*, the symbol meant many things: it was the pointed arrowhead of the hunter; the wing of the bird that passes between the worlds; the mountain in whose

shadow they all lived. It was the mark of her clan. Ren-*ya*'s mother had needled the same sign on Ren-*ya*'s hand with charcoal and spit when she was a day-old grizzling.

'What are you staring at?' the girl said.

With her heart thumping in her throat, Ren-*ya* pulled off her glove and held her hand up.

The girl's face drained of colour as she glanced from Ren-*ya*'s palm to her own. 'What does it mean?'

The insult of this puny *white-eye* having anything to do with Ren-*ya*'s family turned her stomach. She spat her disgust into the fire. 'It means we are sisters.'

ONE OF THEM

Sisters? Bela didn't know what to think. When she was growing up, she'd dreamed of having a brother or a sister, but she never expected it would be someone like this extraordinary person.

All she could do was stare at the girl. Her lips were parted and Bela could see that her small white teeth had been filed to sharp points. But it was her eyes that were truly astonishing. They were two dark pools, completely black from one corner to the other, huge and wide-set like the eyes of a deer. Bela remembered the dream she'd had, the woman who ran ahead of her on the train, who'd turned to show a face like Bela's, but with eyes as strange and black as Ren-*ya*'s.

After a long silence, Ren-*ya* said, 'The idea that we

share the same mother is not believable. I cannot bear the thought.'

What she said was harsh, but her voice was beautiful. It swooped from a height and fell, rose again like music. Her speech was full of clicking sounds she made with her tongue against her teeth. It was a language Bela had never heard before, and it still surprised her that she understood every word. 'How is it we can understand each other?'

Ren-*ya* dismissed the question. 'I told you before. This is not the waking world. Spirit speaks to spirit without need for language.'

She grabbed Bela's hand and examined the tattoo again. 'This is what does not make sense. Mam would never have anything to do with any *white-eye*.'

Bela shook her head. 'My father was a good man . . .'

'That is hard to believe.'

'Well, it's true . . . and I'm here now, aren't I?'

Ren-*ya* eyed her suspiciously. 'So you took the totem from her?'

'No! I took it from my uncle. He stole it, years ago. He's the one who has invaded your world and brought the people you call *white-eyes* here. He has many fighting men and weapons against which yours will be useless . . .' Bela dropped her head, unable to meet

Ren-*ya*'s unfathomable eyes. 'He's the one who murdered our mother.'

Ren-*ya* said nothing and only stared into the flames of the fire. But Bela could taste the same searing, burnt-hair fury that she herself had felt when she found out.

After a long time, Ren-*ya* lifted her chin. 'Who is this man? What is his name?'

'Viktor Novak.'

She spat into the fire. '*Viktonovak*,' she repeated, running it together like a single word. 'Tell me what happened. Tell me everything.'

Bela held out her hands. 'Untie me first.'

Ren-*ya* looked reluctant, but she cut the sinew and Bela began her story. 'My father found a woman's body in the ice . . .'

All afternoon, Bela talked and Ren-*ya* listened. When Bela told about her mother's incarceration, the professor bleeding her to a slow death, Ren-*ya* turned away and stared into the fire again, but she said nothing. She didn't interrupt until Bela told her how she'd climbed into the professor's room and taken the totem.

'Why did you not kill him?' Ren-*ya* said. 'You stood over him, the man who murdered Mam, who you say murdered your father too . . .' She trailed off, shaking her head in disbelief.

'I couldn't do it,' Bela said.

'Then you are weak,' Ren-*ya* replied.

'But I would've been punished.'

'For what? He killed your parents. He owes you his life.'

'Where I come from, it doesn't work like that.'

Ren-*ya* sucked her teeth. 'How can it be any other way?'

Bela folded her arms across her chest. 'You just don't understand.'

'No,' Ren-*ya* said, narrowing her black eyes. 'It is *you* who do not understand. You say my people are facing death. Nothing would have stopped me from cutting his throat.'

A tense silence stretched out between them. Eventually, Ren-*ya* sighed. 'My people say that the past is cooked, but the future is still raw. Tomorrow we will travel to my village. We must return the totem to Hebera, our shaman, and warn my people of *Viktonovak*'s plan.'

She went outside and came back with a joint of meat that she cut into chunks and strung on to a pointed stick. She pulled her hood off as she worked, revealing long auburn hair that was braided close against her head and threaded with black feathers. Bela studied her profile. From this angle, she could see the girl's eyes were unusual in another way. Instead of facing forward, they curved slightly round the side of her face. Despite how different she looked, Bela had seen the way she licked her lips, the way she lifted her chin and sucked air into her mouth. To Bela, it felt like a wonderful thing to find another person who tasted the world, just as she did.

'How did I get here?' Bela said.

Ren-*ya* laid the skewered meat across the fire, balanced on two Y-shaped sticks. 'I found you lying in the snow. There were no tracks leading up to you; it was as if you had fallen out of the sky. I dragged you back here on the sledge.' She took the skewer from the fire and, when it was cool enough, pulled a piece off and handed it to Bela. 'Eat.'

'Thank you,' Bela said. 'In fact, I should be thanking you for a lot more than –'

'Just eat,' Ren-*ya* said.

Bela took a small, experimental bite. It didn't taste bad. 'What is it?'

'Deer.'

'Did you catch it yourself?'

Ren-*ya* spread her hands and looked around as if to say, *Who else would've done it?*

'Why don't you live with your people? Why are you here all on your own?'

'I can look after myself.'

It wasn't a proper answer, but Bela didn't doubt her. She could see the collection of stone tools laid out neatly by the fire, a quiver of arrows and a bow propped against the side of the shelter. The shelter itself was small. There was barely enough room for both of them to lie down, and the roof was too low to stand. Even so, Bela could see it was practical and well made. The fire in the middle was contained within a circle of stones and the smoke escaped through a hole in the roof. The hides that covered the floor made it comfortable and kept it warm. Yet everything was suffused with a taste like dried flowers. Bela knew that desolate flavour very well: loneliness.

When they'd eaten, Ren-*ya* said they should cure

the rest of the meat, ready for the journey. She set up a wooden frame over the embers of the fire and gave Bela one of her sharp-sided stone tools. 'You can help.'

Bela turned the stone over in her hand. 'What am I supposed to do with this?'

Ren-*ya*'s eyes widened. 'You must have cured meat before?'

When Bela shook her head, she spat in the fire and muttered, 'What do these people eat?' She snatched the stone blade from Bela and showed her how to carve thin slices of meat from the bone. As Ren-*ya* worked, Bela's gaze was drawn to her quick fingers, the deep pits and scars that covered the backs of her hands.

Ren-*ya* looked up. 'See? Now you try.'

Bela was out of her depth. Ren-*ya*'s hands had moved far too fast for her to grasp the technique, but she took the blade and did her best to cut the meat as Ren-*ya* had done. 'When did our mother leave this place?'

Ren-*ya* shot Bela a look that was full of anger. '*My* mother. And she did not *leave*: she was wrenched from this world.'

'How? What happened?'

'She could hear her body in the ice whispering to her, telling her she had been found. She said she knew what was to come. One night she was there and the next morning when I woke she was gone. We thought she would soon return, to lead us all back home, but after many, many moons had passed we gave up hope.'

The stagnant taste of Ren-*ya*'s loss filled the shelter, but Bela didn't know what to say or do to comfort her. 'Don't you have any other family?' she said. 'What about your father?'

'Dead.'

Bela was about to say that was another thing they had in common, but then Ren-*ya* said: 'He was killed by a sabretooth.'

'Oh . . . I'm sorry.'

Ren-*ya* shrugged. 'I do not remember him. I was a grizzling when it happened.'

'Isn't there anyone else?'

Ren-*ya* didn't reply. Instead, she leaned over and adjusted Bela's hand on the stone. 'Hold it like this or you will have your fingers off.'

Bela thought she was avoiding her question, but after a minute she sighed and said, 'I am here to complete my initiation. I must live alone through the *long winter*.' She shrugged. 'I have trained for it all my life. It is who I am.'

Bela couldn't help envying the girl's certainty. Unlike her, Ren-*ya* knew exactly who she was. 'And when you finish, then what?'

'If I live to be fourteen, I will have proved I am worthy to be a full member of my clan. I will no longer be Ren-*ya*, *little* Ren. I will be Ren, a grown-up. At least, that is what *should* happen.' She cast her eyes down. 'Mam disappeared many moons ago and after that I stopped going back to my people at the end of the winter.'

'Why?'

'Because I can never grow up. I have been thirteen years old since my people came here from the waking world.'

Bela stared, open-mouthed. 'But that was ages ago, wasn't it?'

Ren-*ya* frowned. 'No one can count the number of winters that have passed.'

'Then why don't you get older?'

'Because my body in the waking world is still a child.'

Bela started to ask another question, but Ren-*ya* cut her off and pointed at the meat. 'You are slicing it too thick.'

Bela turned her attention to the meat, doing her best to cut it thinner. It was obvious that Ren-*ya* didn't want to be questioned, but the way she lived was unlike anything Bela could have imagined and she was overcome with curiosity. 'You must get lonely out here.'

Ren-*ya* tutted. 'Take the fat off, or the meat will spoil.'

Bela knew she'd touched a nerve. No one wanted to admit they were lonely and she let the conversation drop. She concentrated on cutting the meat while Ren-*ya* rubbed the strips with salt and draped them on the wooden frame over the embers of the fire to dry.

It was a horrible job. As the meat warmed, the shelter filled with the sweetish stink of congealed blood. That and the pile of stripped white bones at Bela's feet made her feel sick. But she didn't complain. She was determined to show she could pull her weight.

Hours later, Bela finished slicing the meat. Although she hadn't done it as thinly as Ren-*ya*, she was pleased that she'd managed to complete the task. 'Maybe you could teach me other things,' she said to Ren-*ya* as they hung the last strips over the frame together.

'Like what?'

Bela shrugged. 'How to build a shelter and light a fire, how to hunt . . .' She trailed off when she saw the look of disbelief on Ren-*ya*'s face.

'You cannot do *anything*, can you?' she said. 'Without me here, you would die.'

'You'd be just as helpless if you came to my world.'

Ren-*ya* sucked her pointed teeth. 'But we are not in

your world; we are in the spirit world of my people, the Last.' She looked at Bela thoughtfully. 'Are there many of you, back in the waking world?'

'In my family?'

'I mean, are there many of your kind?'

'Human beings?' Bela glanced at Ren-*ya*. Human wasn't the right word. If this girl wasn't human like Bela, then what was she? 'You mean . . . other people like me?'

'Yes, *white-eyes* like you.'

She glanced up into Ren-*ya*'s huge black eyes. She must look as strange to Ren-*ya* as Ren-*ya* did to her.

'Show me on your fingers,' Ren-*ya* said.

'There are far too many for that. There are millions of us.'

Ren-*ya* looked back at her blankly. 'What is "millions"?'

Bela thought for a moment. How to explain? She was reminded of her father's journal, his description of her mother when he first brought her to Wilder House. The way she constantly looked about her, unable to comprehend the world she'd woken into.

'There are as many of us as stars in the sky.'

Ren-*ya*'s face fell. She turned away and looked into the fire. 'We came here to escape your kind. Now they will all come here and kill us.'

'No . . .' Bela began, but however much she wanted to say Ren-*ya* was wrong, she knew her uncle and his mercenaries were here somewhere in Ren-*ya*'s world. It would be a lie to say there was nothing to fear.

Ren-*ya* looked over at her. 'Why has *Viktonovak* come here? What does he want?'

Bela hesitated. It was not a question she had asked herself, but she'd seen the professor's laboratory; she'd seen the way he manipulated those around him. He wanted everything to be under his control. He liked to line his specimens up, cage them, label them, experiment on them, and she could only think he meant to do the same to Ren-*ya*'s people. 'He wants to rule this world and everyone in it.'

Ren-*ya* took the totem out of her pocket. She held it up and its earthy, metallic flavour filled the narrow space. The crystal orb seemed to smoulder in the firelight as it spun backwards and forwards on its strap, sending golden points of light darting across the walls of the shelter. 'He wants this back, does he not?'

Bela nodded and Ren-*ya* handed the stone to her. 'Here, keep it safe.'

Bela was surprised.

'Why are you giving it back to me?'

'You brought it here, so you should carry it.' She cast her eyes down. 'I took it from you in anger. I should not have done.'

Ren-*ya* watched closely as Bela hung the totem round her neck. 'And you, *Bela* –' It was the first time Ren-*ya* had used her name, and she curled her tongue clumsily round the unfamiliar word. 'Why are *you* here? What is it that *you* want?'

This time, Bela didn't hesitate. 'I came to find out about my father. He used the totem to come here, but Viktor Novak stole it from him when he was asleep . . . What would've happened to him, do you think?'

'His spirit would be stuck here,' Ren-*ya* said. 'No living spirit can pass between the worlds without the totem.'

Bela's heart quickened. 'So . . . could he have survived?'

Ren-*ya* snorted. 'If he was anything like you, he would be dead in less than a day.'

Bela hung her head. 'Oh.' She thought for a moment and raised her head again. 'But could there be traces of him, some signs that he was here?'

'Maybe. If you could

find them.' Ren-*ya* peered at her. 'But he is dead. Why does this matter to you?'

'He's part of me, and until I find out what happened to him, I feel as if I cannot know who I really am.'

'Oh, I can easily tell you that. You are one of them. A *white-eye*.' Ren-*ya* narrowed her black eyes. 'None of you belongs here.'

WHITE-EYES

At first light, they packed the dried meat, a water carrier and as many rolled-up animal hides as they could carry. Before they left, Ren-*ya* took a piece of the meat and laid it on the ground.

'What are you doing?' Bela asked.

'I am making an offering to the guardian spirits of my people, Eagle, Raven and Crow.' She poured a little water on to the snow. 'I am reminding them that I am a living spirit and asking them to help us on our journey.'

She handed Bela a pack to carry. 'Come.' She turned and set off, leading the way through the trees.

Ren-*ya* had given Bela a caribou tunic and leggings to wear under her parka and she was soon glad of them. She had never experienced cold like this before.

It burned its way deep into her lungs, and when she breathed out, a smoky cloud unravelled in the freezing air, leaching her body heat away breath by breath.

Ren-*ya* was walking a few yards ahead, her shoulders pulled up to her ears, and Bela realized she was doing the same. The cold turned a person inwards. It had to be endured alone, in silence.

As they walked along, Bela's thoughts returned to what Ren-*ya* had said about her father, how he would have been stuck here in the spirit world after the totem was taken from him. Eva had said the same about the professor. For the first time since she'd arrived, she thought about what must be going on back at Wilder House. How long would it be before Krol and the servants noticed something was wrong? They would quickly find that she and Arno had gone. It wouldn't be long before the door to the professor's quarters would be broken down and they'd find him there asleep, the totem gone.

And what about here in the spirit world? The professor would have suddenly found his precious totem gone and realized he was trapped. In her mind's eye, Bela saw him pacing about, wondering who could've taken it. She knew it wouldn't take him long to work it out, and she couldn't help smiling, imagining the moment when he realized he had underestimated her, that it was Bela who had the totem now.

After an hour of walking, they emerged from the forest at the edge of a ridge. The ground fell steeply away and they could see for miles around. To the east, a vast forest stretched as far as a distant range of snow-patched mountains.

Ren-*ya* pointed to the west. 'Over there. That is where my people live.'

A frozen plain dotted with trees stretched before them. Beyond the plain, sunlight sparkled on a faraway sea. Bela could just make out a group of offshore islands, a smudge of grey that seemed to hover above the horizon. It suddenly hit her that there was absolutely nothing here. No roads, no houses, no people. It was a wilderness.

'What is this place?' she said.

'It is the spirit world of my people, the land where the ancestors live.'

'It looks like the waking world.'

Ren-*ya* nodded. 'It is a perfect reflection of the waking world at the moment we left. But it does not taste the same, does it? Here, every rock, tree and bird is made of spirit, even our own bodies. We are all an echo, a whisper of that other world . . . Come, we must go.'

She led the way along the edge of the ridge as it dipped down, finally guiding them out on to the plain where the trees were bent under the weight of snow. They struck out towards the sea.

'How far is it?' Bela asked as they slogged on.

'Half a day.'

'And when we get there?'

'Hebera will want to know the totem has returned. My people have been sickening since Mam disappeared, and the totem with her.' She gave Bela a hateful look. 'And now I know why, since the totem has been in the grasp of a *white-eye* and not one of my people.'

Bela decided it was the wrong moment to point out that she, a so-called *white-eye*, was still in possession of the stone. 'So why is it so important?'

Ren-*ya* turned back to her. 'The totem is the doorway between the worlds. It holds the prophecy the spirits made, that our descendants shall thrive in the waking world. We have lived in the land of the dead for all this time, and, when the totem was lost, my people also lost their belief, their hope . . . It is not good to live without hope.'

She walked on and Bela hurried to catch up. 'So, after we take the totem back, what then?'

'You can stay with them. They will look after you. I cannot be expected to do so any longer.'

Ren-*ya* quickened her pace again and Bela was forced to speak to her back. 'What about you? Will you go back to the shelter?'

'No. This man, this *Viktonovak*, I will find him.'

'How?'

'I will go to the Big Forest. My people say his warriors leave tracks as deep as a herd of mastodons. They will lead me to him.'

'And then what?'

Ren-*ya* stopped and turned back to her. 'I will do what you could not. I will kill him.' She turned on her heel and set off again.

After a few hours of walking, they stopped to rest and eat.

'I want to go with you,' Bela said.

Ren-*ya* was sitting on the ground, her back propped against the trunk of a tree. 'What for?' she said through a mouthful of food.

'I'm your sister.'

'*Half*-sister,' she snapped.

'I could help.'

Ren-*ya* laughed. 'We both know you would be more of a hindrance.'

Bela was tired of hearing how useless she was. 'Without me, you wouldn't even know his name. *I* know all about him. You don't even know what he looks like.'

Ren-*ya* took a swig of water. 'He is a *white-eye* – that is all I need to know.'

Bela huffed the breath out of her mouth. 'It's what our mother would've wanted.'

Ren-*ya* stopped with the water bottle halfway to her lips. 'What?'

'She said her daughter would avenge her.'

Ren-*ya* eyed her for a moment. 'She did not mean *you*. She meant *me*.'

'How do you know?'

'*I* am the first-born, the older sister.'

'You might've been born first, but you're still only thirteen, the same age as me.'

Ren-*ya* didn't reply. She only sucked her teeth and spat into the snow, but Bela knew she'd touched a nerve.

Bela put one foot down after the other, following in the tracks Ren-*ya* had made. The more she thought about it, the angrier she got. What made Ren-*ya* think she was the only one who could avenge their mother? *I'm perfectly capable of doing it*, Bela thought. She'd climbed over the roof of a four-storey house and taken the totem all alone, hadn't she? She hadn't needed anyone's help then, and she didn't need it now. But her mind kept drifting back to the landscape she'd seen that morning from the top of the ridge. It was a brutal world of rock and ice and snow. She couldn't survive here alone.

It was all right for Ren-*ya*. She'd been *taught* to survive. She knew what to do. Bela focused on her sister striding out ahead of her. She thought differently, looked different and yet . . . There was something about Ren-*ya* – her self-assurance, her insistence that she was right. She was infuriating, but, somewhere inside, Bela knew that she was just the same.

Suddenly Ren-*ya* stopped. She pointed down at the ground, where a trail of deep bootmarks led in from the east. '*White-eyes.*'

'How many?' Bela said.

'Fifteen, maybe.'

'But you said they were on the other side of the forest.'

'They *were*. Now they will be looking for you and the totem.'

They followed the trail. After a while, the tracks converged in a clearing. Deeper depressions in the snow showed where shelters had been pitched, and there was a patch of blackened snow where the fire had been. Ren-*ya* bent down and sniffed at a set of animal tracks. 'They have their wolf-like beasts with them.'

Bela went over and looked at the tracks. 'Dogs,' she said.

Ren-*ya* searched round the edges of the abandoned

camp and came back, carrying a hurricane lamp. She tapped on the glass and sniffed at it. 'Tastes strange,' she said. 'What is it?'

'It's a light. Put it in your pack – it'll be useful.'

They followed the tracks out of the clearing, but soon the trail turned in a new direction.

'They are heading towards the sea, towards my village,' Ren-*ya* said, and Bela could taste her fear. They hurried on.

When they were within shouting distance of Ren-*ya*'s village, they stopped. Everything was quiet. 'Too quiet,' Ren-*ya* said. Bela strained her ears. All she could hear was the tinkling of ice crystals forming in the freezing air, the background hush of the sea.

Ren-*ya* went ahead. The trees thinned out and at the edge of the forest they came to Ren-*ya*'s village, or what was left of it. The place was deserted. Fine threads of smoke rose from the gutted ribs of the shelters. The hard-packed earth was strewn with the shafts of arrows, stone tools, shreds of animal skin. It was as if someone had turned the people's homes upside down and tipped the contents out.

Ren-*ya* wandered, head bowed, between the

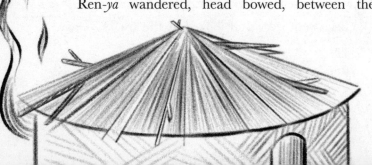

smouldering remains. She flashed a resentful glance at Bela. '*Your* people did this.'

'They're not *my* people and you know it.'

Ren-*ya* kicked at a pile of scorched animal bones among the ashes. She looked ready to continue the argument, but was interrupted by a loud crack in the distance. It was followed by another and another in a regular rhythm. The two girls stood, listening. Sometimes there was a pause, and then the cracking noises would start up again.

'What is it?' Bela said.

'Sounds like someone felling trees.' Ren-*ya* sucked the air in through her pointed teeth. '*White-eyes*,' she said. 'I can taste them.' And when Bela lifted her chin, she too caught the familiar flavour: bitter, like the pith of an orange. She'd always wondered why other people had a slightly different flavour to her, and now she knew the answer.

They moved quickly in the direction of the strange sounds, running from tree to tree. The cracking grew louder, echoing through the forest. Suddenly everything went quiet.

Ren-*ya* dropped to the ground, pulling Bela down next to her. 'Come with me.'

They crawled on their bellies to the edge of a clearing, where three men stood round a tree that had just been felled. One man leaned on the long handle of an axe, giving orders, while the other two looped ropes round the fallen tree. When it was tied up, the three of them carried it away. Bela and Ren-*ya* crept after them.

The men dragged the tree to the edge of the forest and out on to a shingle beach, where they joined another group, who were lashing the trees together. Other people were milling about and Bela counted eleven men, although there were four large shelters pitched behind the beach, enough to house more.

Ren-*ya* lifted her chin. 'See that *white-eye* there? What is that he has?'

Bela followed her gaze. At the edge of the camp, a man sat on a tree stump, warming his hands in front of a fire. Next to him a long black stick was propped against the stump. Bela screwed up her eyes. It was too regular, too perfectly straight to be a stick.

Her heart sped up. The man had a gun.

THE SHAMAN, HEBERA

Bela explained to Ren-*ya* what the weapon was and how it worked.

Ren-*ya* thought for a moment. 'We must tell my people what we have seen. They will have retreated to the islands. Come, I have a boat hidden further down the beach.'

They crept back into the forest and tracked a few miles along the coast, only coming out of the cover of the trees when they had gone far beyond the burnt-out village.

Bela followed Ren-*ya* across a shifting dune of sand and scrub and out on to a narrow shingle beach. As soon as Bela emerged from the dunes, a freezing wind drove into her. She bowed her head and made her way to the shoreline, clambering over rocks and skirting the clear saltwater pools that glimmered in between.

At the edge of the sea, Bela shaded her eyes and looked out. She held her breath in awe. Huge icebergs floated in the fast-moving waters of the channel between the islands and the shore. The nearest was only about thirty yards from the beach. It was colossal, but despite its size it was finely carved, deep blue in its hollows and crevices. It was like a cathedral of ice.

The huge berg shifted in the water. It was top-heavy, undercut at the base. It rose out of the waves on a crest of foam and listed heavily to one side. It stayed there for a moment, impossibly balanced, until there was a crack like a gunshot and the vast berg rolled over. With a deafening boom, it fell back, the sea boiling round it as it settled into the waves. Gradually, the berg was sucked away by the current and, as it glided past, Bela heard an eerie symphony of shrieks and groans. It sounded like the despairing cry of human voices in that lonely place.

'Come on! Hurry up!' Ren-*ya* was already some way down the beach and Bela had to run to catch up with her.

Ren-*ya* led them to the foot of a cliff, where she crouched down. 'Help me with this.'

Together they rolled a rock away from the entrance

to a low cave. Ren-*ya* reached in and tugged out the pointed prow of a kayak. Between them, the girls dragged it down to the shoreline.

Bela kneeled down and peered inside. It was no more than a fragile frame of wood covered in hide so thin she could see light through it. She glanced out to sea. That stretched piece of skin would be the only thing between her and all that cold grey water. 'Are you sure it will take both of us?' she said.

Ren-*ya* patted the side of the boat. 'Of course. I learned to hunt seal in this. Mam was an expert at sniffing them out.'

Bela caught Ren-*ya*'s dark gaze. *Mam.* It was a name that spoke of familiarity, of love, and Bela felt the weight of sadness and envy pressing down on her. It reminded her that Ren-*ya* had actually lived with their mother, learned from her, while Bela had no memories, nothing. All she had was a faceless paper image frozen behind glass.

Ren-*ya* must have tasted her feelings. 'Come,' she said in a softer voice. 'Time to go.'

She dragged the boat into the surf and held it while Bela got in, then she pushed it into deeper water and climbed in herself. Wielding the double-ended paddle with firm, confident strokes, she drove the kayak out into the channel.

Bela looked over the side. At first she could see the sand and pebbles on the bottom, but they soon reached a cliff edge on the sea floor and the water beyond was dark and impenetrable. As they crossed into the deeper water, the kayak was pulled round in the current and dragged swiftly along the coast. Ren-*ya* had to put all her effort into keeping the prow pointing out to sea.

As they approached the shore of the nearest island, Bela saw a huddled group of children standing on the beach, waiting for them. The eldest, a girl of about eleven or twelve, came out into the surf and pulled the kayak up on to the shingle.

Bela felt her blood rushing through her body. Would the Last be happy to see her?

Ren-*ya* got out of the kayak and the two girls solemnly pressed their palms together. Then, the formal greeting over, the girl threw her arms round Ren-*ya*. The smaller children ran forward too and hugged her legs. 'You have been gone so long, Ren-*ya*!' they shouted. 'Where have you been?'

But the older girl looked over Ren-*ya*'s shoulder. 'Who is this?' she said, peering inside Bela's hood. When she saw Bela's face, she cried out and drew a blade from her belt.

Ren-*ya* caught her hand. 'Faram-*ya*! Put your knife away!'

The girl fought, struggling to free herself. 'Why would you bring a *white-eye* here? Have you not seen what they have done to our village?'

'She had nothing to do with the attack,' Ren-*ya* said.

Angry tears streamed down Faram-*ya*'s face. Her mouth was set and her gloved hand was curled tight round the blade. 'Who is she then?'

'She is my –' Ren-*ya* stopped and Bela saw the struggle playing out across her face. She saw that Ren-*ya* was ashamed of her, ashamed to admit they were sisters. It wounded her as much as any knife.

'She is Nagar's daughter,' Ren-*ya* said at last, pushing Faram-*ya*'s blade aside. 'Go on, lead the way. We must see Hebera at once.'

Faram-*ya* cast a final dark look at Bela and reluctantly tucked the blade into her belt. She gathered the smaller children around her protectively and made her way up the beach and into the trees.

Ren-*ya* and Bela followed to a hillside where overhanging rocks formed the entrance to a cave. Inside, a fire burned, and Bela could see people huddled together in the light of the flames. They turned towards her as one, raised their chins and tasted the air.

At the back of the cave, a kind of platform had been built out of rocks and covered in furs. Lying on it was an old woman with a raven crouched behind her. She raised a hand when she saw Ren-*ya* and beckoned for her to approach.

'Hebera.' Ren-*ya* pressed her palm against the shaman's and kneeled down next to her. 'What happened? Are you hurt?'

Hebera waved her concern away. 'It is only a

flesh wound, but it could have been much worse. The *white-eyes* have a weapon we have never seen before. It sounded like thunder.'

'A gun,' Bela said.

Hebera's black eyes came to rest on Bela's face. 'Help me up,' she said to Ren-*ya*.

As Ren-*ya* lifted her, Hebera gritted her teeth against the pain. When she was sitting, she gestured for Bela to come closer. 'Take off your glove.'

The old woman inspected the tattoo on Bela's palm. 'Nagar's child,' she said. She reached out and touched Bela's cheek, her hair. 'I have been waiting for you. I have seen you in the *smoke* . . . You have the totem?'

Bela pulled the crystal orb out of her parka and held it up. A hush fell over the cave and all eyes turned to look. The crystal cast a concentrated glow on the upturned faces of the Last. Some were so overcome by the sight of it they covered their faces with their hands and wept.

One by one, Hebera called each of them forward to hold the shining stone, and the cave filled with the sound of whispering.

Bela's skin prickled. 'What's that?'

'It is our bodies in the waking world,' Hebera said. 'They commune with us and make us strong again.'

Last of all, the shaman held the totem in her hand herself. '*Usta*,' she chanted, and a new sound joined the chorus of whispered voices. To Bela, the flavour that filled the cave was like the lime-green growth of pine needles in the spring. It was the same flavour she'd held on her tongue throughout the journey to Siberia, when she'd thought a whole new life was beginning. It was the taste of hope.

Hebera's face had been grey, but now there was colour in her cheeks. 'It does us good to be in its presence again. The totem holds the prophecy the spirits made so long ago, that one day our clan shall return to the waking world. When Nagar and the totem were lost to us, we lost our belief in that prophecy, and our hope with it.'

When Hebera tucked the totem back inside Bela's parka, Bela said, 'I brought it here for the Last. You must take it back.'

But the shaman shook her head and repeated the words Ren-*ya* had said to her before. 'You brought it here and you must be the one to carry it.' She leaned in close and the raven behind her stretched its neck and leaned in too. 'You have a lot of your mother in you,' she said. 'I can taste her in your spirit. But are you with us or them?'

'With you,' Bela said. 'I've come to learn who I am

and avenge my mother's death.'

Ren-*ya*'s head whipped round. 'No! I am the one who will avenge her!'

Hebera covered Ren-*ya*'s hand with her own. 'This girl is Nagar's daughter too.' She turned to Bela. 'Now, Nagar's child, tell me what you know of the *white-eyes*' weapon.'

She listened carefully as Bela did her best to explain how a gun worked.

In turn, Ren-*ya* asked about the attack on the village. It had come a day ago – two warriors had been killed and Hebera and three others wounded.

'They approached from upwind,' Hebera said. 'We knew they were coming, but there were so few of them. We thought they had come to talk and I sent warriors out to meet them, in peace. We didn't know about this weapon –' she looked at

Bela – 'this *gun* that wounded us from far away.' She closed her

black eyes. 'I do not know how we will survive without Eagle and Crow to help us. Now only Raven remains.' She stretched her hand out and stroked the feathers of the bird behind her. 'I do not know what happened to Crow, but Eagle has turned against us.'

Ren-*ya* glanced up, horrified. 'How do you know?'

'I have seen it in the *smoke*.' Hebera was silent for a moment and then she threw her hands up. 'And where is Malor when he is needed? If he was here, he would say we should have fought them long ago.' She shook her head and sighed. 'Maybe he was right. Now they are even more powerful than before.'

Ren-*ya* glanced round the cave. 'Where is Malor?'

'He went off to the Big Forest alone, moons ago, and never came back.'

'You mean . . . he is dead?' Ren-*ya* said.

'Most like.'

Ren-*ya* hung her head. 'So we have lost our guardians and

now our greatest warrior.'

The shaman stretched out a hand and touched Ren-*ya*'s cheek. 'I am sorry. He was your teacher and I know what he meant to you . . . When we mourn for our dead, we will remember Malor's bravery too. And then you will rest. Tomorrow, at first light, you must go.'

'But I want to stay and fight,' Ren-*ya* said. 'The *white-eyes* are felling trees, building boats. They will be here soon.'

'And this time we will be ready,' the shaman said. 'But you have a graver task, Ren-*ya*. The *white-eyes* must not get the totem – so tomorrow you must leave. Now go. Eat, rest.'

When Ren-*ya* got up, Hebera held Bela back. 'I would speak with you, Nagar's child.'

Ren-*ya* went to sit with the others by the fire. Hebera watched as Ren-*ya* hugged and clasped palms with them. 'She can be difficult, yes?'

Bela shrugged. 'I don't suppose I'm any easier.'

Hebera smiled. 'Good. You show loyalty to her and she will do the same for you.'

'I don't know. She doesn't trust me.'

The shaman raised an eyebrow. 'It is hard for her to suddenly learn she has a sister. And to imagine the mother she lost, loving another daughter.'

'My mother never had the chance to love me.'

Hebera shook her head. 'She had you for less than twelve moons, but she loved you deeply.'

'How can you know that? She died in another world.'

'I have seen it in the *smoke*, child. I have seen glimpses of it all, how the *white-eye* stole her blood and found the way into our refuge. Now you stand before me, I understand all the pictures I have seen.' The shaman and the bird drew their heads together, as if a silent conversation was taking place between them. 'You are lost, child. What is it you seek?'

It was uncomfortable to mention a *white-eye*, but Bela couldn't miss the chance to hear what Hebera knew. 'I came here to find out what happened to my father. Have you seen anything about him in the *smoke*?'

She shook her head. 'But the spirits will help you. They have brought you here and they will guide you.'

Hebera leaned towards Bela and tasted the air. 'You are lonely, child, but you do not have to be alone.' She gestured to the others sitting round the fire. 'They do not yet trust you, because of the way you look, but when we have mourned our dead, I will speak for you. If all agree, you will become a member of our clan. It is what Nagar wanted –' Hebera turned Bela's hand over and traced the outline of the tattoo on her palm – 'or she would not have marked you as she did.'

Bela looked up into the shaman's face, desperate to hear more. 'What was she like?'

'You should ask Ren-*ya*.'

'It's not easy to ask her anything.'

Hebera laughed softly. 'Well, this is the story I told at her remembering. When Nagar was a child, she was chosen to become a warrior, but when the time came for her initiation she refused to set out for the *long winter*. Her father scolded her. *Nagar*-ya, he said, *I have promised you to Raven as a warrior. You will shame me if you do not go. Bow down before Raven and ask her forgiveness.* But Nagar-*ya* refused. *You bow down before Raven*, she said, *since it was you who mistook me for a warrior when I am clearly a shaman.*

'The people were angered by her lack of respect and they sent her out into the snow with no blade or hide to build a shelter. They said, *Come back when you have learned some manners and you are ready to bow down and accept your destiny.* But Nagar-*ya* refused again. *I am no Raven-warrior and no Crow-healer either. I am a shaman, meant for Eagle, and tomorrow, to show their displeasure, the spirits will put out the sun and the day will be as night.*

'The people laughed at her and drove her off with sticks, but the next day what Nagar-*ya* had said came to pass. The people were terrified. They ran out to search for her, fearing the wrath of the spirits if they had let her die in the snow. She was found, wrapped up against the cold in the wings of a golden eagle.'

Hebera smiled, remembering, and shook her head. 'There could not have been a clearer sign that Eagle herself was protecting her.

'After that,' Hebera continued, 'Nagar became my apprentice. But she was not always easy to teach. She was quick to laugh and quick to forgive, but she was often outspoken, and never knew when it was time to remain silent.' She turned to Bela and gave her a wry smile. 'How I wish she was with us now, the bravest shaman the Last have ever had.'

Late in the afternoon, the Last brought their dead into the cave and laid their bodies out. One by one, each member of the clan stood and told a remembrance. The man and woman who had died were both warriors, and many of the stories were of their bravery in battle or the hunt. But as Bela listened, she thought it was the ordinary remembrances, about the things they loved, the things that made them laugh or cry, that brought them back to life.

When the storytelling was over, Hebera was helped to her feet. She called Bela to her and turned her to face the Last. 'Yesterday we lost two members of our clan. Today the spirits have sent us Nagar's child.' She held up Bela's hand so all could see the tattoo on her palm. 'I will vouch for her, but each one of you must decide whether to accept or spurn her.'

Bela was sent outside while a decision was made. The Last would discuss it and then vote.

After more than an hour, the clan filed out of the cave and went into the trees. Ren-*ya* came out last. She went to walk past Bela, but Bela caught her hand. 'What happened? Have I been accepted?'

Ren-*ya* kept her eyes averted. 'Ask Hebera. I must help to gather wood for the funeral pyres.'

Bela went inside the cave and Hebera called her to sit beside her. 'I am sorry, child. Most voted to accept you, but everyone must agree.'

'How many were against it?' Bela asked.

'Just one.'

No doubt it would have been wrong for Hebera to say who had voted against her, but Bela didn't need to be told.

It was Ren-*ya*. She knew it.

She dipped her head so that Hebera wouldn't see

the tears that filled her eyes. It was a pointless gesture, since the taste of Bela's hurt hung heavy in the air between them. 'Thank you for trying,' she managed to say before she left the cave.

Outside, people were returning from the trees, carrying armfuls of branches. Some stared at Bela while others smiled at her sympathetically, which only made her feel worse. *They pity me*, she thought, *because even my own sister doesn't want me.*

Bela wandered away from the cave and went back through the trees to the beach. She'd had enough of being stared at. She slumped down on a rock and watched the clouds behind the faraway mountains turn pink in the setting sun.

They'd voted for her because Hebera had asked them to, but none of them really wanted her here and she knew very well why. To them, she must look like an enemy, a *white-eye* killer.

She let her head fall into her hands. For the first time, she questioned her decision to come to the spirit world. Her father was dead, and, whatever Hebera said about the spirits, how could she find out what had happened to him in this vast wilderness?

Being here with the Last was unbearable. All her life, she'd known she was different, that she didn't belong. Now she'd found her mother's people, her sister.

But the truth was that she didn't belong here either. She wasn't a *white-eye* and she wasn't one of the Last. She was something in between, neither one thing nor the other. She thought of Ren-*ya*, her clan gathered round her. That would never happen to Bela. There was no one else like her in this world, or any other. She was alone.

ACROSS THE NARROW STRAIT

When Bela raised her head again, night had fallen. On the horizon, a single point of light shone in the darkness. The first evening star.

As she watched, another point of light sprang to life, and then another. With a horrible jolt, Bela realized they couldn't be stars – they were moving.

She got up and ran back to the fire where Ren-*ya* was sitting, surrounded by her people.

'Ren-*ya*!' Bela shouted. 'They're coming!'

Suddenly all was uproar. The Last ran back and forth, shouting and gathering their weapons.

Ren-*ya* kneeled down next to Hebera. 'Let me stay with my people and fight.'

'No.' The shaman nodded towards Bela. 'You must

go with her.'

'But she cannot fight or hunt or even build a shelter. Why do I have to be the one to look after the *white-eye*?'

Bela stepped forward. 'I'll go alone.'

Hebera shook her head. She took hold of Ren-*ya*'s shoulders and turned her to face her. 'Listen to me. This girl has risked her life to bring the totem home.'

Ren-*ya* spat on the ground.

The shaman's knuckles whitened as she tightened her grip on Ren-*ya*. 'Do you mean to defy me? Your shaman?'

For a long moment, Ren-*ya* held Hebera's gaze, but then she looked away. 'No, I will not disobey you. Where should we go?'

Hebera let her hands slip from Ren-*ya*'s shoulders. 'You must take the totem far away from here. After that, who knows? We must trust the spirits to guide you.'

Ren-*ya* picked up her pack, ready to leave.

'There is one more thing I must tell you.' Hebera's black eyes glazed over. 'Something I have seen in the *smoke*. Each of you must face a test. Each of you will make a promise. Each of you will make a sacrifice for the other.'

Hebera fell back, exhausted. When she spoke again, it was not clear whether she was talking to Ren-*ya* or Bela. 'All our futures depend upon you and the choices you will make. Protect your sister and the totem with your life. Now go.'

Ren-*ya* and Bela ran down the path to the beach. The kayak was there, listing in the surf. Ren-*ya* stored the backpacks in the prow and held the boat while Bela got in. She pushed off, climbed in and began to paddle directly towards the shore.

'What are you doing?' Bela said. 'You're going straight towards them!'

Ren-*ya* threw an angry look over her shoulder. 'I know what I am doing! The current is strong here between the island and the mainland and there is no way I can paddle against it. I am going to let it take us out and then we will go round behind the island, where the current is weak.'

Bela looked towards the mainland. She could see the lights strung out in a line where the land met the sea.

Her heart seemed to shrink inside her. 'Can they see *us*?'

As if in answer to her question, the curved edge of a huge moon appeared between the peaks of the mountains, and their little boat was illuminated in the bright splinter of light that arced out across the sea. Ren-*ya* pushed the kayak's prow on through the water, breaking the reflected moon into undulating strobes of silver and black that rippled away into the gloom.

The kayak reached the middle of the flow and Bela sensed the tug of the current and the cut of the wind at her back as the boat turned and was pulled away up the channel. She looked over her shoulder. Now the moon's beam shone on the *white-eyes*. She could see people climbing on to rafts and pushing out into the channel. On one of the vessels, a white sail bloomed into the wind.

Ren-*ya* looked back. 'What is that?'

'It's a sail. It's made to catch the wind.'

Behind them, the first raft caught the breeze and took off from the shore. Bela could see another sail flapping and unfurling and a second raft was pulled into the channel. Borne on the wind and pushed along in the flow of the current, the two rafts seemed to fly across the sea towards them.

There was nothing Bela could do but watch. The moon rose, escaping the mountains, and the narrow, glimmering arc it shed on the water spread out across the bay. Ahead of them the ghostly shapes of icebergs loomed out of the night.

The rafts were closing in and the one in front was bending its sail towards them. On either side stood a man with a long oar and, at the back, another manned the tiller. Their voices travelled over the water and Bela could hear their shouts as they struggled to hold the line across the flow of the current and the wind.

'Hurry!' Bela said. 'They're coming up on our side.'

Ren-*ya* glanced back. 'I am already going as fast as I can!'

The kayak couldn't match the speed of the wind-powered vessel. It came level with them, then edged in front, all the time travelling towards them on the diagonal.

'Look out!' Bela shouted. 'They're trying to cut us off!'

When Ren-*ya* didn't turn to look, Bela leaned forward and shook her shoulder, making the kayak list dangerously from side to side.

'Keep still!' Ren-*ya* said. 'You will capsize the boat!'

The raft was close enough now that Bela could see the oarsman's gritted teeth as he held the tiller firm against the drag of the water. Ren-*ya* tried to get away, turning the kayak back towards the island, but their pursuers adjusted their line and bore down on them. One of them stood on the nearside, crouched at the ready. He held a hooked pole out across the water towards the fleeing kayak, and it seemed to Bela that time slowed to a shuddering chain of horrifying moonlit images.

When the raft was almost upon them, Ren-*ya* turned the kayak hard, slipping behind the raft as it sped across their bow. But the man lurched to the end of the craft and reached out with the boathook. There was a thud as it hit the kayak and bounced along its length. The hook caught on the lip and the boat was wrenched round, dragged sideways before it straightened into the wake of the raft.

The kayak was forced down into the waves and Bela screamed as a freezing rush of black seawater flowed over the top of the boat.

Ren-*ya* drove her paddle flat into the current and the man leaned back, struggling to keep his footing against the drag. Suddenly Ren-*ya* pulled her paddle out of the water and the kayak shot forward. She dropped the tip, catching the man on the side of his head with the blade. He cried out and dropped the boathook into the sea.

The kayak was set free and the raft
sped away from them, heading straight
towards the huge icebergs that floated
in the channel. The three men aboard
struggled to control the vessel with oars
and tiller. When this failed, they fought
to take down the sail. One man raised
an axe. There was a sharp snap as
its tether was cut and the sail was
released, billowing out in the wind.

But they were too late. The current drew the raft on towards the sheer face of a towering wall of ice. It struck the berg and broke up, throwing the men into the sea.

Bela looked back. The other vessel was coming up fast. With renewed vigour, Ren-*ya* dug her paddle into the water and struck out, hugging the coast of the island, so close to shore that the bottom scraped against the seabed. She guided the kayak across the tip of the headland and out of the sea channel. When they were on the other side of the island and free of the current, Ren-*ya* stopped paddling and let the kayak drift.

The raft couldn't follow. Its sail had been pulled in and tied down to avoid the fate of the other vessel, but without the wind they had no power. They were left at the mercy of the current, which pulled them along the sea channel, in the opposite direction to Ren-*ya* and Bela's little boat.

A moonlit figure stood on the edge of the raft, and Bela caught the flash of her pale face as she drew back her hood. She turned her face to the sky, her dark silhouette picked out starkly against the great ice-mountain that loomed behind her. She raised her arms and spread her cloak wide. And then the cloak seemed to change, to transform itself into wings. As the raft smashed into the iceberg, Bela saw a huge bird shoot up into the sky. Her eyes followed the bird until it was lost to sight in the darkness of the night.

'That was Eagle, wasn't it?' Bela said and Ren-*ya* nodded.

Bela shuddered. Eagle was the spirit who had claimed her mother as a shaman, yet she was also the one who had betrayed the Last. Bela had only glimpsed the spirit's shrouded figure as their boat escaped across the narrow strait. But Eagle had seen Bela too and she could feel a connection between them now, a piercing light roaming the labyrinth inside her head.

With deep, even strokes, Ren-*ya* turned the boat and paddled away from the island, but she was soon too tired to go any further. Together they dragged the kayak out of the sea and hid it behind some rocks on the beach. Without stopping to rest, they slogged across the ice, heads bowed against the wind, to the forest's edge, where they made camp for the night.

BELA'S TRICK

Ren-*ya* and Bela woke before dawn. They sat in silence in the makeshift shelter they'd thrown together the night before, chewing on a bit of cured venison while they waited for the sun to rise. Through a gap in the animal hides, Bela could see the glowing embers of their fire, and, beyond that, nothing but the deep darkness of the forest.

'Will they come after us?' Bela said.

'Not in the dark, but they will not be far behind.'

'What shall we do?'

'Find *Viktonovak* before he finds us.'

'And then what?'

Ren-*ya* shrugged. 'Kill him, of course.'

Ren-*ya* had a way of making everything sound simple. 'But he has men,' Bela said. 'And guns.'

'No one said it would be easy. We may fail, but we must try.'

A harsh chattering in the branches made both girls look up.

'It's a magpie,' Bela said.

Ren-*ya* put a piece of the meat in her fist and the bird hopped down to her hand. Bela watched the bird eating and wondered if it was the same one she'd dreamed about back in her own world.

'Good morning, Mr Magpie,' Bela said. 'How is Mrs Magpie?'

Ren-*ya* looked confused. 'Why do you say that?'

'Where I come from, one magpie means sorrow and two means joy. So, if you see a magpie on its own, you say hello to ward off the bad luck.'

Ren-*ya* shook her head. 'That makes no sense. Magpies are often alone in winter. You have to wait until they nest in spring to see a pair.' She turned to the bird and stroked its head. 'It is good you are here. You can show us which way to go.'

Bela threw her hands up. 'So my saying hello is nonsense, but now you're asking a bird which way we should go?'

Ren-*ya* smiled. 'Yes, because he knows.'

'How can he?'

The magpie stopped eating and cocked its head to one side.

'See?' Ren-*ya* said. 'I expect he is wondering how you could question him when he saved your life.'

'What do you mean?'

'It was the bird who found you, who led me to your body.'

Bela made a silent apology to the magpie. This was not her world. She must accept things were different here.

A breeze began to blow and Ren-*ya* lifted her chin and stuck out her tongue. 'We must go,' she said.

At once, the bird took off and flew ahead of them through the trees. Bela and Ren-*ya* followed.

They walked all morning, only stopping for a few minutes for food and water. Here the trees were spaced far apart. Heavy drifts had fallen between them and, with every step, Bela found herself knee-deep in snow. Ren-*ya* said they had to keep going, that their pursuers were not far behind. Bela knew she was right. She could taste them on the breeze too, but she was worn out from the constant walking and the cold and she began to fall behind.

Ren-*ya* waited further ahead with hands on hips and a sour look on her face. 'Do you want them to catch up with us?'

'Of course not,' Bela said, fighting for breath.

'Well, hurry up then!'

They travelled on through a sparse-growing forest of pine and larch and, towards midday, they emerged at the foot of a towering cliff stretching as far as the eye could see in both directions.

'Why have you brought us here?' Ren-*ya* said to the magpie.

In answer, the bird flew ahead, leading them along the line of the cliff until they came to a narrow gorge where a river, now frozen, had cut its way deep into the rock. The bird flew directly into the gorge and was soon lost to sight.

'Does he want us to go down there?' Bela said doubtfully.

'We cannot.' Ren-*ya* pointed at the ground. 'Look at these tracks.'

It was rocky there with little snow and Bela couldn't see anything. 'What tracks?'

Ren-*ya* rolled her eyes. 'Are you blind? A herd of mammoths passed through here this morning. Look.' She showed Bela where the surrounding branches had been snapped off, the places where the snow was thicker and the outline of huge footprints could be seen.

'If we go into the gorge,' Ren-*ya* said, 'we are

bound to come across the herd.' She pointed to another scuffed area on the ground. 'They have calves with them and will be dangerous.' She thought for a moment. 'No. We must climb the cliff or we will be trapped between the *white-eyes* and the mammoths. I will find the easiest place to climb up.'

While Ren-*ya* peered at the cliff face, an idea came to Bela. 'Ren-*ya*? You said the *white-eyes* are clumsy?'

She nodded. 'They have no idea how to move about the forest.'

'Would they recognize mammoth tracks?'

'They are hard to miss.'

'For you, maybe, but I didn't see them. Perhaps they won't either.'

Ren-*ya* turned to Bela. 'What are you thinking?'

Bela explained her idea and, after a few minutes, Ren-*ya* agreed.

First, they cut branches from a pine tree and brushed away the most obvious signs of the mammoth herd. Then they rubbed juniper berries on their skin, masking their scent, and crept quietly into the gorge. They deliberately walked between the rocks where there were patches of thick snow and their tracks would be visible.

They travelled beside the river bed for an hour before they came across the herd. There were nine adults and two calves. Bela had seen an elephant once, a sad, overweight specimen in the Kraków zoo, who ate nothing but doughnuts and had only one tusk. These magnificent beasts did not compare. They were twice the size and covered in long red fur. As they grazed, they swung their heads from side to side, clearing snow from the vegetation with their huge tusks.

Bela and Ren-*ya* doubled back, now keeping to the rocks so that no new tracks would be made. When they were out of sight of the mammoths, they climbed the side of the gorge and tracked along the edge of the cliff until they were above the grazing herd. They hid themselves behind a large rock overhanging the gorge and waited.

Every few minutes, Ren-*ya* and Bela would lift their chins and taste the breeze that blew off the plain. They nodded at each other. The *white-eyes* were getting closer, but would they fall for Bela's trick?

At last they appeared from among the trees, six of them, strung out in a line across the narrow floor of the canyon. Their eyes were trained on the ground and, when they reached the place where the girls' tracks suddenly stopped, they searched around, scratched their heads and had a loud argument about what to do next.

'Now,' Ren-*ya* said. 'Before they realize they have

been tricked and climb out.'

Between them they managed to push the large rock over the edge and sent it crashing to the river bed below. But the herd didn't panic. They drew together, the adult mammoths surrounding the calves protectively.

'It is not enough,' Ren-*ya* said. 'We have to get them running.' To Bela's surprise, she fixed an arrow to her bow and took aim. The arrow flew through the air and hit one of the adults on the rump. It bounced off harmlessly, but the creature raised its trunk and let out a terrifying bellow. A shock wave of panic travelled through the herd. They raised their tails and trunks and began to move back down the gorge as a group, picking up speed as they went. The ground trembled as the enraged herd thundered along the narrow river bed.

Bela and Ren-*ya* followed along the cliff edge, yelling at the tops of their voices, keeping the animals on the move. From their vantage point, Bela could see the advancing herd and, round the bend, the professor's men.

The *white-eyes* could hear the trumpeting calls of the mammoths, feel the shaking of the ground. Some of them looked up and caught sight of the girls above them on the cliff. Bela saw their shocked faces, their looks of disbelief as the mammoths appeared.

The *white-eyes* ran, but it was too late. The herd ploughed into them and the fleeing men disappeared under the feet of the stampeding mammoths.

ONE OF US

That night they camped in the hollow between a stand of ancient pines. Ren-*ya* was in a good mood after the defeat of the *white-eyes*. 'Did you see their faces?' she crowed.

'Yes, I saw them,' Bela said. 'I feel as if I'll never be able to *stop* seeing them.'

Ren-*ya* nudged Bela and grinned, showing her pointed teeth. 'I was glad they had a chance to be truly terrified before they were crushed.'

Bela shook her head and turned away.

Ren-*ya* lifted her chin and tasted the air. 'What is the matter with you?'

'What happened today was merciless. I can't get it out of my mind.'

'Why?' Ren-*ya* prodded the fire with a stick. 'Those *white-eyes* showed no mercy to my people. You think they would not do the same to us?'

'It still doesn't feel right.'

Ren-*ya* spat into the fire. 'I always said you were weak.'

Weak. Ren-*ya* had taunted Bela with that word before and it lit a spark of anger inside her. 'How can you say that? It was my idea to start the stampede in the first place.'

'Exactly! We should be celebrating a great victory! We should be dancing on the bones of our enemies, but all you do is mope. You care too much for those *white-eyes*.'

'Of course I care. They're people, human beings, just like you.'

Ren-*ya* gave her a sly smile. 'Just like *you*, you mean.'

Bela threw her hands up in frustration. 'That's not fair! You know very well I'm on your side, not theirs.'

Ren-*ya* turned away from Bela and stared into the fire. 'So you keep saying, but how can I ever trust someone like you?'

Bela grabbed Ren-*ya*'s shoulder and twisted her round. 'It doesn't matter what I do, does it? You'll always find a reason to say I can't be trusted. I'll never be able to prove myself to you.'

Ren-*ya* shrugged her off. 'The only thing you have proved is that you will never be one of us.'

Bela had been rejected all her life, but it had never felt as painful as it did now, and when she replied her voice shook. 'My whole life I've wished I had a family. I've longed for a brother or a sister. I never expected it to happen, and I certainly never expected to find a sister who would turn out to be someone like you. I've done everything I can to show I mean well and to try to understand you . . .' Bela was suddenly struck by the truth of this and all the hurt she felt came tumbling out. 'But now I see I'm not like you and I never will be. If it means gloating over the deaths of other people, then I *never* want to be one of you.' She left Ren-*ya* by the fire and went to the shelter alone.

Ren-*ya* threw more wood on the fire and pulled a fur across her shoulders. She was cold, but there was no way she was going inside the shelter until that white-eyed girl was asleep. Ren-*ya* could not understand her behaviour. Was it too much to expect a bit of celebration after such a victory? The defeat of the *white-eyes* was the sort of story Ren-*ya* could tell the grizzlings on long winter nights for years to come.

Of course, it had been Bela's idea. It was a clever trick, and Ren-*ya* had even started to think the girl was not as useless as she'd first imagined, but now she seemed to care more about the comfort of their enemies than the survival of Ren-*ya*'s people.

That thought brought her up short. What had happened to them all? She remembered the wind-powered rafts of the *white-eyes*. Had any of their vessels made it across the strait between the mainland and the island? If only she had been there, fighting shoulder to shoulder with the warriors, facing down their enemies together. Hebera would have let her stay if it hadn't been for that girl.

The night had been still, but as Ren-*ya* sat there, thinking, a sudden wind blew up, stripping the flames away from the embers of the fire. Just as suddenly, the wind dropped and the smoke rose straight up into the sky once more.

Ren-*ya* pressed her hand to her thumping heart. Something was going to happen; she knew it. Something was out there in the darkness, just out of sight, just beyond the glowing light of the fire. Ren-*ya* got to her feet and unsheathed her blade. She lifted her chin to taste the air.

The long-lost flavour of herbs and crowberry settled on the back of Ren-*ya*'s tongue. 'Is it you?' she said. 'Is it really you?'

A hooded figure emerged out of the night. She came into the circle of firelight, moving silently, as only the dead can do. She was cloaked in the splayed wings of a golden eagle, and, when she took off her hood, Ren-*ya* gazed upon her mother's face. She raised her hand, and although the fire burned between them, Ren-*ya* felt the touch of cool fingers on her cheek.

*

'Bela! Wake up!'

Bela opened her eyes. It was still night-time and the only light came from the fire that burned outside. 'What's happened?'

Ren-*ya* turned and pointed towards the fire.

'What?' Bela said. 'Is there someone out there?'

'There was . . . but she has gone now.'

'Who?'

'It was Mam.'

'How could it be?'

'Come, let us get warm by the fire and I will explain.' Ren-*ya* crawled out of the shelter and Bela followed.

She glanced round the campsite, but everything looked exactly as it had before. 'Perhaps you were dreaming?'

Ren-*ya* spat on the ground. 'Asleep, awake, what does it matter?' She held Bela by the shoulders, forcing her to look her in the face. 'She was here. I saw her.'

'So what happened?'

'I was sitting by the fire where you left me. Suddenly I felt something, here.' She pressed her fist to her heart. 'And then I caught the taste.' Ren-*ya* lifted her chin and drew in a deep breath, as if she was remembering the moment. 'She came from among the trees and sat down opposite me by the fire.'

'Did she say anything?'

Ren-*ya* nodded. 'She told me I had done you wrong.'

Bela gazed at her sister's face glowing in the light of the fire. It felt to her then that she and Ren-*ya* and the circle of flames were the only things that existed in the whole world.

Ren-*ya* sighed. 'It is not easy, but there is something I must tell you. When we were back on the island with my people –'

'You were the one who voted against me.'

Ren-*ya* glanced up in surprise. 'How did you know?'

Bela shrugged. 'It wasn't hard to guess.'

'Well . . . Mam said I must put it right.' She took a leather pouch from her pocket.

'What's that?' Bela said.

'We call it the *smoke*. It was made from the ashes of the fire that burns in the Cave of the Spirits, mixed with a drop of blood from every member of the clan.' She closed her fist round it. 'It is the most precious thing I own.'

Bela remembered Hebera talking about the *smoke* and she watched with fascination as Ren-*ya* tapped a tiny quantity on to a flat-topped stone. 'Do you eat it?' she asked.

Ren-*ya* laughed. 'No. We put it in the fire and

breathe it in.'

'Does it hurt?'

'Not like you are thinking, although sometimes the truth is painful.' She gazed at Bela. 'The ceremony should have been carried out by Hebera, in the presence of the whole clan, but I cannot help that now.' She sucked her teeth as if the next bit was hard for her to accept. 'The spirits say you must make the *smoke* part of you and become one of us.'

Bela kept her eyes lowered. *One of us.* Even Ren-*ya*'s reluctance could not ruin the moment. It was the first time anyone had said such a wonderful thing to her. 'What do I do?'

'First, we must add a drop of your blood.' Ren-*ya* took out her knife. 'Give me your hand.'

Bela tugged off a glove. Before she even had a chance to shut her eyes, Ren-*ya* whipped the blade lightly across the tip of her index finger and a small bulb of blood welled out of the cut. Ren-*ya* turned Bela's hand over and squeezed a drop on to the ashes.

'Now it is time to meet the ancestors. They will gift you a truth, an answer you have craved.'

'I have to ask a question?'

'No need to ask; the spirits know.' Ren-*ya* led her back inside the shelter and made her lie down. 'When the *smoke* comes to you, breathe it in. But remember:

what you taste and see and hear is for you only.'

Bela watched as Ren-*ya* went back outside and sprinkled the *smoke* into the flames. 'Her name is Bela,' Ren-*ya* said. 'She has come to take her place among us.' At once, tall flames jumped up, white at the base and blue at the tips. There was a sound like a sigh and thick smoke wound its way out of the fire and into the air. The purplish pall drifted into the shelter and Bela breathed it in.

Bela woke to the touch of a hand on her cheek. When she opened her eyes, she found herself in the forest, surrounded by many people.

Bela's gaze darted from face to face. All were unknown to her but one, the woman who had woken her. She had black eyes and a face Bela had seen in her dreams – her mother.

She took Bela's hand and held it up, palm outwards for all the others to see. 'One of us,' she said, and the others all replied the same.

Each of them came forward and touched Bela's hand before turning and disappearing into the trees, until only Bela's mother remained. 'Come,' she said. 'I will show you the truth.'

She led Bela to the edge of the forest, where a great house stood.

Bela recognized the many beautiful windows, the overlapping tiles like the scales of a snake, but there was no scaffolding covering the walls and the house had a look of newness about it. Bela realized it was Wilder House as it had been in the past. She turned to ask her mother whether she should go in, but there was no one holding her hand now. Mam was gone.

The door swung open by itself and Bela went inside. She climbed the sweeping staircase and went into a room at the top, where a woman was lying in bed, cradling a newborn in her arms. There was a boy standing by her bedside, but neither of them noticed Bela. They couldn't see her; she was like a ghost.

The mother showed the baby to the boy. 'Isn't he beautiful?'

'I hate him!' the boy said. 'He's as ugly as a turnip. Let's get rid of him and go back to how it was before, just the two of us.'

His mother was angry. 'He's your brother and you will learn to love him.'

Now the scene changed and Bela found herself in a dimly lit room. In the middle was a cot with a sleeping child inside. As she watched, the door opened quietly and the boy, a little older now, came in. He crept to the cot and peered down at his little brother. The boy held a pillow in his clenched fists and a terrible look passed across his face.

Bela knew what he meant to do and cried out to stop him, but the boy could not hear her, and she was drawn away, pressed against the ceiling in the corner of the room. She could only watch in horror as the boy lowered the pillow over the face of the sleeping child.

Suddenly the mother rushed in and grabbed the baby, took him in her arms and kissed his little face. 'How could you do such a thing?' she said to the boy.

But the boy did not cower or cry. He only said he wished his mother had come in a little later.

His mother turned her back on him. 'You are no child of mine.'

She had the boy locked up in a place where there were no windows, no light. Now the boy cried and called out for his mother. 'Help me!' he screamed. 'I'm afraid of the dark!'

But no one came to let him out.

As Bela watched, the boy grew old, until his face had hardened into the grey and hateful one of the man she knew. Any goodness her uncle had ever had was gone, and his withered heart held nothing but his yearning for revenge.

THE CHILD WHO IS
BOTH YOU AND ME

Bela woke from her vision to the sound of a screaming storm.

She could just make out Ren-*ya*'s hunched outline. Her huge black eyes looked back at her, shining in the gloom. 'It is only the wind,' Ren-*ya* said. 'There is nothing to fear.'

Bela tried to sit up, but her whole body was stiff, as if the cold had calcified her bones.

Ren-*ya* helped her up. 'Everyone feels a bit weak after their first time with the *smoke*. Here –' she passed Bela the water bottle – 'have something to drink.'

Bela gulped down a few mouthfuls. The water had thickened in the cold and was full of tiny ice crystals that burned her throat and made her cough.

'Hot root tea would help,' Ren-*ya* said, 'but I cannot light a fire in this blizzard. We are stuck here until it blows over.'

'How long will that be?'

'Who knows?'

'Shouldn't we get going? Won't the professor's men be following?'

Ren-*ya* made a dismissive sound in her throat. 'They have lost our trail and will never find it now.' She pulled aside the flap of hide covering the opening to the shelter and a freezing blast of snow blew in. 'Not even a wolf goes hunting in this.' She closed the flap again, tucking the edges of the hide together to keep the weather out. 'All we can do now is eat, rest and do our best to stay warm.'

Ren-*ya* shared out the meat and berry cake that Hebera had given them. As they ate, neither spoke and the only sound was the shrieking of the wind, but Ren-*ya*'s eyes did not leave Bela's face. When they had finished eating she said, 'Tell me about your home.'

Bela shrugged. 'I didn't think you were interested.'

Ren-*ya* gave her a tight smile. 'Well, what else is there to do during a storm but tell stories?'

Bela thought for a moment. It would be difficult to get Ren-*ya* to understand how different the world had become since the Last had walked the earth tens of thousands of years before. 'So much has changed,' she said. 'Remember that morning when we left for your village? We looked out across the plain and all we could see was wilderness. No roads, no houses, no people.'

Ren-*ya* raised an eyebrow. 'What are *roads*?'

Bela sighed. Explaining was going to be even harder than she'd thought. She decided to try a different approach. 'If you want to go somewhere, what do you do?'

Ren-*ya* rolled her eyes. 'I walk there.'

'Well, in my world it's different.'

Ren-*ya* looked at her as if she was mad. 'You have legs but you don't walk?'

Bela smiled. 'We *do* walk, but we don't *have* to.' She wondered how to begin to explain the many ways people could travel in the waking world. Maybe, if she started with something that would be familiar to Ren-*ya*, such as horses, she could work up from there. 'It all began when people realized they could go further and get to places faster if they rode on the backs of horses, or in carriages pulled along by many horses. It meant we could travel a long way very quickly, and we made roads – hard, flattened strips of land that the wheels of the carriages could move easily on.'

Bela glanced at Ren-*ya* to see if she was listening and understanding. Her already wide black eyes had widened even further and Bela was pleased that she at least had her attention. 'We have things called trains,' she continued, 'which go faster than a horse can gallop and which belch out smoke from the hot fires burning in their bellies. We travel across the oceans in ships that carry hundreds of people, driven by engines with the power of thousands of horses . . .' She stopped and looked at Ren-*ya*. 'Is this making sense?'

Ren-*ya* blinked a few times and wrinkled her nose. 'What is a horse?'

Bela couldn't help laughing. 'I thought you would know.'

'Maybe you are trying to explain the wrong things. Tell me about your people.'

Bela stopped laughing. 'I have no people.'

'What about the ones who looked after you when you were small?'

'My great-aunt?'

'Was she good to you?'

'I hardly saw her. She handed me over to the servants to be looked after.'

The shelter was narrow and Ren-*ya* was no more than a few inches away, looking directly into her face. Bela found she couldn't hold her gaze any longer and dipped her head. 'There's no point trying to explain,' she said. 'You wouldn't understand. You'll just say my life was easy.'

'Tell me.' Ren-*ya* reached out and lifted Bela's chin until she was forced to look into her eyes again. 'I will do my best to understand.'

'But I'm not sure what to say. It's not a story I have ever told before.'

'Why not?'

'No one has ever asked.'

'Then I am honoured to be the first to hear it.' Ren-*ya* crossed her legs and got herself comfortable, drawing a fur round them both. 'I am ready,' she said. 'Begin.'

'My story isn't like yours,' Bela said. 'I never had to fight or learn to survive. I lived in a warm and

comfortable house. I wore fine clothes and there was always as much food as I could eat . . . yet I have been cold and hungry all my life.'

Ren-*ya* tasted the air. 'You mean the cold and hunger of the heart?'

Bela nodded. 'You see, they were ashamed of me . . .'

As Bela told her tale, the furious storm outside intensified. Although it was the first time of telling, she held nothing back. She told about the punishments she had endured whenever she licked her lips, stuck out her tongue, put something in her mouth. She told how she learned to conceal her strange talent, to taste the world secretly, to cover the tattoo on her palm.

At times, the storm was so fierce, she had to raise her voice and shout, or stop altogether as the howling gusts battered the walls of their little shelter. But even when her words were lost to the roar of the wind, the taste of her anger and her grief filled the space between the sisters. Bela made Ren-*ya* understand. She made her feel the agony of growing up with the dreadful stink of shame. How it clung to every word, how it attached itself to her, burrowed its way inside. How, in the end, it became a living part of her and she was truly ashamed of herself.

'You've always known who you are, Ren-*ya*,' Bela

said. 'You are meant for Raven, a warrior and a hunter. But I have had to hide my true nature. I've had to pretend to be something I'm not and I must learn to be who I really am.'

By the time Bela's story came to its end, the storm had exhausted itself. The wind was stilled and fresh snow lay smooth and unmarked on the ground.

For a long time after Bela had finished, Ren-*ya* was silent, running her hands over the fur that covered them. 'Your story is full of pain,' she said. 'And now I understand what Mam showed me last night.'

'Why? What happened?'

'When she sat down with me by the fire, she was carrying a bundle that she unwrapped in front of me.'

'What was it?' Bela said. 'What was inside?'

Ren-*ya* bit her lip. 'It was a grizzling. She showed me the palm of its little hand and I saw the mark and I knew the child had to be me. But then the baby opened its eyes.' She glanced at Bela. 'They were brown, white-rimmed, and I realized the child was you.'

There was a pressure on Bela's heart that made it hard to breathe. 'So which was it? Was the child you or me?'

'It was both of us – do you not see?'

'But what does it mean? Did she say anything?'

Ren-*ya* dipped her head and for a moment she was quiet. 'She said you are strong; only now I see she did not mean the strength of the body, but the strength of the heart. She told me we needed each other, that together our strength would be unbreakable. This is the meaning of the child who is both you and me . . .' She picked at the blanket with her fingers, pulling out the tufts of fur. 'Do you forgive me for not tasting this truth from the beginning?'

Bela nodded.

For a moment, Ren-*ya*'s gaze roved across Bela's face. 'Your eyes are white-edged like theirs, but your hair is the same colour as mine and you have a way of frowning when you think that reminds me of Mam.' Ren-*ya* took her hand. 'I will no longer say those others are your people.' She pressed the clan mark on her palm against Bela's. 'You are truly one of us. The Last are your people now.'

LITTLE SISTER

The next morning, Bela woke in the shelter, gripping Ren-*ya*'s hand in her own. Their fingers were interlocked, the tattoos on their palms still pressed together.

Ren-*ya* said there was no time to rebuild the fire, so they ate cold leftovers and packed up as quickly as they could. But when it was time to leave, the magpie was nowhere to be seen.

'Which way shall we go?' Bela asked.

'Towards the Big Forest, that's where *Viktonovak* and his men will be.' Ren-*ya* dipped her head. 'I do not like it over there.'

'Why not?'

'There are many beasts. Cave bears, wolves,

sabretooths. There are also many spirits, and not all of them are good.'

Bela shivered. If Ren-*ya* was worried, then she knew it really must be dangerous.

They set off and walked all morning, on and on. They could have been going in circles for all Bela knew. She saw no living creatures and heard no sounds except their own, although the many tracks they came across told a different story. Ren-*ya* pointed out a deep channel cut into the snow made by the body of a deer. It had been brought down by wolves and dragged away into the trees. She seemed to be able to read those marks of death like runes.

The trees around them were taller and closer together, but Bela was so cold and tired she hardly noticed. She kept her eyes on the ground and put her feet down in Ren-*ya*'s footprints, where the snow had already been compacted by her boots.

In the afternoon, thick clouds gathered. It began to snow heavily and the going got harder. The falling flakes joined the earth to the sky and the whole world turned white. One minute, Ren-*ya* was right there, a few steps in front of Bela. The next time she looked up, her sister had disappeared.

Bela stopped. 'Ren-*ya*?'

She peered ahead. The dark shapes of trees loomed

out of the whirling snow, but there was no horizon, no landmarks and now no footprints to tell her which way to go. She shouted Ren-*ya*'s name again, but there was no reply.

She stumbled around for a while, trying to find the trail, but the ground was flat and there were no shadows to help her pick out a shallow bootprint.

Bela ran her tongue over raw lips. She was desperately thirsty, but didn't want to stop, even for a moment, in case Ren-*ya* got too far ahead. A heartless voice in her head told her it wouldn't make any difference: she was already lost.

Fear and imagination began to work on her. She thought she heard a sound behind her and spun round, half expecting to see one of the creatures Ren-*ya* had named running towards her out of the blizzard. But there was nothing, only her thudding heart and her own disappearing footprints in the endless snow.

She called out again, 'Ren-*ya*!' Her voice sounded dead and flat in the falling snow.

Panic crawled in her throat. She couldn't survive out here in the forest on her own and the sly voice returned to taunt her: *She'll get tired of waiting. She'll leave you behind.*

Bela blundered on. Her senses were drawn tight and even the sound of her own footsteps frightened her. She couldn't help thinking they masked the approach of something or someone following behind and she almost cried out when two ravens fell soundlessly out of the sky and landed in the trees. They ruffled their feathers and sat hunched in the falling snow, their wings hanging around them like ragged black cloaks.

There was a sound like the crack of breaking wood and the ravens lifted off into the air and flew away. Bela stood still, the blood thumping in her throat. A ripple of movement travelled through the trees at the edge of the clearing and a wedge of snow slipped from the branches with a hollow thud.

Bela held her breath, caught between her instinct to run and the desire to stand her ground and fight.

When Ren-*ya* suddenly appeared from the white-out, the relief made Bela's legs give way, and just like that she was flat out in the snow, crying like a baby.

Ren-*ya* ran over, dropped to her knees. 'Where did you go? Did you not hear me calling you?'

'No,' Bela sobbed. 'I thought you'd left me.' She didn't care how pathetic she sounded.

Ren-*ya* pulled her up. She held Bela's face in her hands and looked directly into her eyes. 'Whatever happens, *suran-ya*, I will not leave you.'

'*Suran-ya*?' Bela said. 'What does it mean?'

'It means "little sister". For our people, it names a sacred bond. It is my promise to protect you, whatever the cost.'

It was the first time Ren-*ya* had spoken of them as sisters without spitting, and instead of the usual flavour of disgust a sweet taste hung in the breath between them. Bela wiped her tears away. 'I make the same promise to you, Ren-*ya*.'

After that, Ren-*ya* walked next to her, talked to her. Later, Bela didn't remember exactly what Ren-*ya* had said, but she would never forget the sound of her high musical voice, her presence at Bela's side.

The clouds lifted a little from the trees and the snow stopped falling. Bela was bone-tired, but somehow she put one foot in front of the other and kept going.

They'd been walking through thick forest for another hour when Ren-*ya* stopped and crouched down to inspect a fresh set of tracks. Even Bela could tell they weren't made by deer.

'Sabretooths,' Ren-*ya* said.

Bela peered at the tracks. She could see there was more than one set. 'Do they hunt in packs?'

Ren-*ya* nodded. 'There are three of them. They came through here a little while ago.'

A sick feeling wedged itself in Bela's throat. She'd

seen a picture of a sabretooth in a book once. The animal had been drawn with its muscular front legs pinning its prey down, its impossibly long canines puncturing the animal's neck.

Ren-*ya* looked up at the sky. 'It will snow again and there is not much daylight left. There are some caves not far from here. We do not want to be outside tonight.' She lifted her bow off her shoulder and nocked an arrow. 'Just to be on the safe side.'

They hurried on as the sky darkened. Ren-*ya* kept looking up at the thick clouds and when the first flakes began to fall she said, 'Good. It is harder for them to track us in the snow.'

From then on, she walked ahead and quickened her pace, but she stayed close and didn't leave Bela behind. From time to time, she stopped and tasted the air, held a finger to her lips as she listened to the deep hush of the forest.

Bela found herself slipping into a strange state. Her mind was far away. She got into a kind of rhythm, one that started and ended with her feet coming down in the snow, lifting, landing again. Her hands and feet were numb with cold and it felt as if her body didn't belong to her any more. Somehow it carried on walking automatically.

She was moving like this, walking half blind, when

she bumped into Ren-*ya*'s back. She'd stopped again to listen. Bela heard it too: a faint howling coming from far away. The breeze brought a wet-dog flavour to her mouth.

Ren-*ya* grabbed Bela's shoulders and shook her out of her trance. 'Listen to me! They have picked up our scent. Leave your pack.' She pointed into the trees. 'Run!'

'But what about you?'

'I will hold them off here. Now go!'

BENEATH THE FOREST FLOOR

Bela ran. Her breath came in searing gasps as she darted between the trees. She could hear the sabretooths calling to each other, closer now as she stumbled on in the darkening snow.

She was exhausted, but terror forced her on. The trees thinned, giving way to a clearing, and here the deep snow slowed her, sucking at her boots. She struggled forward with the cold tearing at her lungs, lurched across the clearing and back into dense forest, where the snow was thinner.

She pushed on, zigzagging between the black trunks of the trees, blindly crashing into low-hanging branches. They seemed to jump into her path out of nowhere, whipping across the naked skin of her face.

Out to her left, she caught something at the edge of her vision. It was huge, at least as tall as she was, flashing black and white, black and white between the trees. It ran parallel to her, no more than thirty feet away, as if it was chasing down something up ahead. And then, like a scene from a nightmare, the creature turned its head. Through the falling snow, she saw the glint of its jaw, its amber eyes like lanterns in the dusk, and she knew it was coming for her.

It slowed, changed course and disappeared among the trees. Seconds later, she heard its panting breath behind her. She twisted round to face it.

The beast slunk out of the trees, its muscles tensed, ready to spring. As the creature leaped, Bela took a step back. The ground gave way beneath her, swallowed her up, and she fell feet first into darkness.

She kept on falling, bumping and sliding against hard earth walls. She threw out her arms, tried to grip the sides of the shaft. One glove snagged on a twisted tree root and for a moment she hung there, while under her feet the earth began to give way again. Her hand slipped out of its glove and she fell until stopped by the narrowness of the tunnel. But the earth around her was loose and moved like liquid, trickling past her until the way below cleared and she was sucked down again. The earth closed over her head like quicksand.

When at last she stopped falling, she found herself stuck, one arm caught above her, the other trapped between her body and the wall, her head wedged into a tiny airspace in the crook of her elbow. At first she felt only relief at escaping the sabretooth – but then she twisted her head to look up, expecting to see a circle of light, the entrance to the tunnel she'd fallen into. There was nothing, only darkness, and Bela realized she'd fallen deep into the earth, far below the forest floor. She was buried alive.

Panic got hold of her and she squirmed, trying to free herself. But she was wedged in the narrow tunnel and moving only shifted the earth around her, making her slip further down in the tight grip of the frozen ground.

Bela fought for breath, coughed dirt up from her lungs and spat it out. She got the urge to struggle again, to scream and cry. But she knew it wouldn't help, and she quietened her breathing and made herself be still and think.

Her situation was hopeless. She had no food or water, and she'd be dead from the cold in a few hours. Already she could feel pins and needles in her arms and legs, a numbness spreading through her body.

She closed her eyes and remembered her sister's face. Ren-*ya* was Bela's only hope and she clung to the promise she'd made. *Whatever happens,* suran-ya, *I will not leave you.*

But her hope was as thin as water. Ren-*ya* might be dead, ripped to pieces by beasts, and even if she'd survived, she could wander around in this wilderness forever and never see the tiny hole in the ground Bela had disappeared into. She imagined the forest above her, the snow falling thickly, relentlessly, filling up her tracks so that no one would ever know where she'd gone.

Time passed. Bela didn't know how much. It was hard to tell when the only measure was the working of her own body. She fell in and out of a shallow sleep, each time waking to the sharp knife of the cold.

Then something else woke her, something scratching away around her feet. The earth gave a little beneath her and she found she could move her foot. There was more scraping and her other leg was freed up to the knee. She kicked her foot and shouted, 'Ren-*ya*!' It had to be her. She'd found her and was digging her out.

But the rank flavour of rancid meat filled the narrow tunnel and the faint, muffled voice that came from beneath her was not Ren-*ya*'s.

'Watch out!' The voice was high-pitched like a child's. 'It's still alive.'

'We've got a big one here!' came the reply. This time, the voice was lower, but it had the same childish sing-song tone.

Bela went very still.

'Ooh yes. It's got boots on though. Hold that lamp up and help me get them off so we can have a proper look.'

Bela moaned as a sharp tug on her leg pulled her further down the tunnel.

'The laces are too tight,' said the high-voiced

creature. 'Give me the blade.'

Hearing that, Bela kicked out as hard as she could and her boot made contact with something soft.

'Ow!'

There was some high-pitched giggling.

'Oh yes, I might've known you'd find that funny.'

'I told you to watch out, didn't I?'

'Just help me over here, will you? Get hold of that foot and keep it still.'

Bela struggled and kicked out with all the strength she had left, but she was held tight. There was another tug on her leg and she felt her boot slip off.

She listened, horrified, as there was an eruption of excited sniggering.

'Ooh, it's a lovely one though, isn't it?'

'We haven't caught a big one like this for a long time.'

That word *caught* made her struggle again and she cried out, 'Please . . . please help me.'

There was a listening silence and then a whisper. 'Did you hear that? It said something again.'

'I don't care what it says, so long as it tastes nice!'

Bela closed her eyes. She told herself she must be dreaming. Her mind seemed to detach itself from her body and the creatures' voices came to her from far away.

She was helpless. Hunger, thirst and exhaustion made her drift back into unconsciousness. The shrill voices beneath her faded and, rather than fight the tiredness that overwhelmed her, she welcomed the escape into darkness.

REN-*YA*'S SACRIFICE

Ren-*ya* positioned herself at the top of a shallow rise, as far from the treeline as possible. It would give her time, she hoped, to reload her bow at least once. She kneeled in the snow, fitted an arrow and pulled the bowstring to her shoulder. For a moment, she was distracted by the thought of Bela. But there was nothing she could do to help her now, and there was no room for anything in her mind but the creatures that were coming for her out of the forest. She drew in a deep breath and remembered what she had been taught by Malor: *Keep your eye on the game.* How she wished her teacher was here to help her now.

They were coming. Ren-*ya* heard them calling to each other. She could taste their acid hunger, and the rising pitch of their howls told her they knew she was close, that they could smell her too.

In those last few seconds, Ren-*ya* made the world narrow until she saw nothing but the dark spaces between the trees. She drew her mind and her breath inwards, focusing everything on her fingers and the tension in the bowstring. Nothing existed for Ren-*ya* now but the swift arc between the arrow and the trees.

She took one of them down as soon as it ran out of the forest. It was a perfect shot. The arrow caught the beast full in the throat and it roared, rolled over, spattering the snow with blood that seemed black in the failing light.

There were two more behind. One peeled off to Ren-*ya*'s right and disappeared among the trees. The other kept on coming through the falling snow.

Ren-*ya* nocked another arrow. Her fingers trembled on the bowstring and she yearned to shoot at once. But she knew better than that and she waited, the blood beating in her ears, for what seemed the longest second of her life. When the beast was almost upon her, she let her arrow fly. It hit the sabretooth in the shoulder. The beast faltered, but its momentum carried it on.

Ren-*ya* put her arms up as it crashed into her. She was knocked off her feet and its weight pinned her to the ground.

The creature opened its massive jaws and went for Ren-*ya*'s neck, but she brought her arm up and its teeth closed round her elbow. Now the massive canines were unable to pierce her flesh, but the sabretooth was huge and muscular. It shook Ren-*ya*, dragging her backwards and forwards in the snow as if she weighed nothing. With her blade in her fist, she brought her free arm up and tried to stab it in the throat. She only managed a glancing blow, but the blade was sharp and it opened a long wound in the animal's neck. The creature roared and, releasing Ren-*ya*, backed away.

Ren-*ya* got to her feet, keeping her eyes on the injured creature. At the same time, she listened out for the other beast, which might circle round and attack from behind.

The sabretooth snarled and opened its massive jaws, ready to leap again, but its eyes flickered as its blood sprayed out on to the snow. It stumbled to its haunches and tried to lick the wound before it went limping back into the forest.

Ren-*ya* reloaded her bow, then she ran, following the tracks Bela had left. Already they were blurring at the edges, filling up with snow. She stumbled on, quickening her pace, realizing the third sabretooth must have gone after her sister. This thought was confirmed when she saw the running tracks coming in from the left, converging on Bela's.

Ren-*ya* shouted out Bela's name as she lurched on through the trees. She was brought to a halt by a gaping hole in the snow. Evening was coming on and it took her a while to find the sabretooth's tracks, heading away. But there were no human footprints beyond that black pit. Bela must have fallen into it.

Ren-*ya* got down on her knees. She couldn't make it out very well in the gloom, but there was a tunnel, almost vertical, leading down into the earth. Around the edge were some thin broken branches. Ren-*ya* could see the raw ends where they must have torn and snapped under Bela's weight. She'd seen traps like this one before. *Sappers.*

Ren-*ya* leaned down and shouted into the tunnel.

'Bela!' She held her breath and listened, but there was no answer.

Suddenly there was a flutter of wings and the magpie landed in a tree nearby. It turned its head sideways and looked down at the entrance to the tunnel.

'The *sappers* have got her,' Ren-*ya* said.

She glanced up at the sky. The last of the daylight was retreating. The evil spirits known as *sappers* slept all day and woke at dusk. They would have found Bela by now.

'They come above ground at night,' Ren-*ya* said to the magpie. 'Do you know where?'

Immediately, the bird took off and flew through the trees. Ren-*ya* followed it to a huge pine with a hollowed-out trunk.

She sat down to wait. The *sappers* would not emerge until the moon was up. But then what? She searched her mind for anything she had been taught about the creatures. She had never seen a *sapper*, but she knew they were curious and loved a game. She remembered her mother saying they were willing to trade.

Ren-*ya* drew the pouch of ashes from her pocket. The *smoke*. It was all she had. She could trade it for Bela, if she was still alive.

Ren-*ya* sighed. She would split the *smoke* and trade half. She took a piece of soft hide from her pocket and opened the pouch, ready to divide the contents, but the magpie flew down with a harsh warning call. The bird landed on her hand, forcing her to stop what she was doing.

'What is wrong?' she said.

The magpie turned its head and she found herself looking into its deep black eye.

Suddenly she understood. Hebera had warned her when the *white-eyes* attacked, only Ren-*ya* had been too angry to bother to listen. Hebera had said both girls would make a promise and a sacrifice, and now Ren-*ya* grasped the shaman's meaning: she must give up the *smoke* in exchange for her sister. She knew in her heart it would be wrong to divide the *smoke*, to try to avoid the test with trickery. The ancestors were demanding she give up everything, all her hopes for the future pitted against her sister's life. Nothing less would do.

Ren-*ya* closed her eyes. She thought of her initiation ceremony, the one she had been waiting for all this time. Without the *smoke*, it could not be completed. If she gave it up, she would be Ren-*ya*, a child forever.

It was the hardest choice she had ever had to make, but there could only be one right answer. Whatever it cost, Ren-*ya* had made a promise. She would not leave Bela while there was any chance she could be saved. But it was more than just a matter of honour; Ren-*ya* realized that, despite their differences, she really had accepted Bela as one of her own people.

Bela was Ren-*ya*'s *suran-ya* now. She *wanted* to make the sacrifice.

For a while, the forest was silent, as dark as earth, and then a huge silvery moon began to rise. A moment later, the glow of a lamp shone from the hollow tree trunk and three ragged creatures came out into the moonlit forest. They stood upright, but they were not human. None of them were much taller than a five-year-old child, but the skin on their faces hung in folds like the oldest crones. Their eyes were huge, luminous and round, and they had curved claws at the end of stubby fingers for digging tunnels.

Ren-*ya* stepped forward and opened her hands to show they were empty.

'Hello, Ugly,' one said. 'What do you want?'

'I have come to trade.'

The spirits looked her up and down. 'Doesn't look like she's got anything worth having.'

'I have something magical in my pack,' Ren-*ya* said. 'Something that deserves a very good price.'

This seemed to pique their interest and they shifted about and peered up at her, snuffling at the air. 'Out with it then, Ugly. Show us.'

'That would be much too easy and there is no fun

in that. There are three of you and you may each have a turn. If you guess right, I will show you.'

The *sappers* tittered excitedly and nudged each other.

'It's reindeer milk, ain't it?' one of them blurted out.

'Shut up, you fool,' said another, slapping him over the head. 'Since when did milk count as magical?'

'Two guesses left,' Ren-*ya* said.

At that moment, the magpie swooped down from the trees and landed on Ren-*ya*'s shoulder.

The three of them eyed the bird and huddled together, whispering.

'Is it your tasty little friend there that you've come to trade?' one asked slyly.

Ren-*ya*'s fingers curled into a fist, but she kept her

voice even. 'Try again, but you only have one more guess.'

The *sappers* started their whispering again. Finally, one said, 'Would it be your beautiful voice then, Ugly? We should like a voice like that.'

'And I suppose you would cut my throat out to get it, would you? No, you have had your three guesses.' Ren-*ya* turned and made as if to leave.

The *sappers* wailed and stamped their feet. 'No, Ugly! We want to see it! Tell us what it is!'

Ren-*ya* sighed, as if reluctant, before opening her pack and laying it on the ground.

The *sappers* crept closer, jaws open, eyes bulging. 'What is it?' they squealed.

Ren-*ya* drew the pouch out of her pack. 'Just one pinch and you will walk with the guardian spirits of this world.'

The *sappers* drew aside and whispered among themselves again. 'What do you want for it, Ugly? We have skins and furs to trade.'

Ren-*ya* shook her head. 'I have plenty of my own. What else can you offer me?'

'We have meat!' screeched one of them.

'A piece of dead rotten meat? What use is that to me?' Ren-*ya* went to put the pouch back in her pack. 'You have nothing I want.'

'Wait!' the *sapper* said. 'It's not rotten. It's fresh, still alive. And it's a big one, like you.'

'Well . . . if it is alive as you say . . .' Ren-*ya* pretended to think about it for a moment. 'I want to see it first. Bring it up here and I will have a look.'

Muttering and giggling among themselves, the three of them hurried away underground. They soon returned, carrying between them a body shrouded in a fur that they laid at Ren-*ya*'s feet.

Her heart pounded as she drew back the fur from Bela's bloodless face. 'What have you done to her?'

'We only took a little blood.' The *sapper*'s tongue flicked out and licked the end of its snout. 'There's plenty left.'

Ren-*ya* pulled off one of her gloves and put her hand to Bela's neck, feeling for a pulse. There it was, faint but regular. 'All right,' she said. 'It is a fair trade.' She threw her precious pouch to the nearest *sapper*.

He caught it and the other two pranced round him, arguing and giggling and trying to snatch it away from him.

'Goodbye, Ugly,' they said as they crawled into the hollow tree trunk and disappeared back underground.

THE CAVE OF THE SPIRITS

As soon as the *sappers* had gone, Ren-*ya* set about making a simple sledge. She took out her stone axe and cut branches from the surrounding trees. She tied two of them together at one end with a length of sinew, bracing them apart with more branches. She hefted the deadweight of Bela's body on to the contraption and set off, dragging it behind her.

It had stopped snowing now and Ren-*ya* could see, above the treetops, the moonlit outline of a great mountain. When Ren-*ya* was small, the Last had lived in the mountain caves, and seeing the familiar jagged peaks, the wind-blasted rock faces, it felt like returning home.

If she could just make it there, she and Bela would

be safe from the hunters of the forest. But now she was beginning to suffer the effects of the sabretooth attack. She was bruised and weakened. Her ankle throbbed where it had been twisted in the fall and she couldn't fully straighten her arm.

She limped on for an hour or more, stopping from time to time to check on Bela. Her skin was icy. She must get her warm soon. But the simple sledge she'd made caught on every rock and tree root, and she cursed herself for leaving the sturdier one behind.

The ground began to rise and the trees thinned out. Ahead of her, the mountain reared up. She scanned the cliff face. The entrance to the caves was not far above her, only three or four times Ren-*ya*'s height. But she'd have to carry Bela and climb up.

She pulled Bela's arm over her shoulder and, with her knees buckling under the extra weight, she pushed herself up to standing and hefted Bela on to her back.

Ren-*ya* climbed, her muscles burning. Several times her legs gave out and she toppled forward and fell to her knees. But each time she got back up and forced herself on, slowly mounting the rocks until she collapsed under Bela's weight at the mouth of the caves. When she'd recovered her breath, she dragged her sister inside.

A little moonlight shone into the entrance, but the further in she went, the darker it got. Ren-*ya* didn't need to see. She knew every twist and turn of the tunnel that took her deep into the heart of the mountain. After a while, the narrow passageway opened into a huge cavern. She rested for a moment, then dragged Bela across the cavern and into one of the smaller side caves. She laid her down and felt around in the dark until she found what she was looking for – a pile of furs and a stack of wood that the Last had left behind.

She covered Bela in furs and set about building a fire. When it was burning, she laid her sister close by to get warm. The taste of woodsmoke filled her senses and there was a faint tang of *white-eye* that she'd noticed on entering the cave. But it wasn't fresh.

She checked on Bela. She was warm and her pulse was strong. She would live.

It was only now that Ren-*ya* could open herself to the terror she'd been keeping at bay. She lay back and stared into the jumping flames, which seemed to take on the shape of prowling hunters, the sharp-toothed grins of the *sappers*. She'd been frightened for herself, but more, she realized, for Bela. Now her *smoke* was gone, but she knew the pain she felt at its loss was the price, the sacrifice, and she was glad to pay it.

Ren-*ya* glanced over at her sister. Since her mother had gone, she'd forgotten how to care, how to love. She had thought this *white-eye* girl had nothing to teach her, but she'd been wrong. Now she knew there was more to living than surviving.

Bela turned her head, mumbled something, and Ren-*ya* went over to her. 'Wake up, Bela.'

Bela's eyes flickered open. 'Where am I?'

'You are safe. It is over.' Ren-*ya* held a water bottle to her lips. 'Drink.'

Bela took several long gulps, then pushed the bottle away and peered into the surrounding darkness. 'What is this place?'

'The Cave of the Spirits.'

Bela looked about fearfully. 'Spirits?'

'Do not be afraid. There are many cave spirits here – hyenas, bears, lions – but they will not approach us.'

'How did I get here?'

'I carried you.' Ren-*ya* took a log from the fire and held it up, illuminating the walls and the low roof that was covered in clusters of white stalactites like fingers.

'Look how beautiful it is.' She threw the log back in the fire and the pale fingers of rock retreated into the gloom.

Bela licked her lips. 'What's that I can taste?'

'*White-eye. Viktonovak*'s men must have been here, but it is old. There is no one now but us.'

A faint noise in the darkness made Bela tense. 'What's that?'

Ren-*ya* cocked her head to one side. 'Only water. These caves were hollowed out by fast-flowing rivers. There are hundreds of caverns, some huge, some too small to stand up in, all joined together by tunnels. Do not go wandering. Those tunnels are a labyrinth. When I was little, I used to go exploring. Mam made me take ochre to mark the walls so I would not get lost. Once, I went a long way in and found a cavern that was cut from the rock by a whirlpool. I would have gone further, but it was a dead end. The way ahead was underwater.'

Ren-*ya* pointed to a darker patch in the blackness behind them. 'When we were many, the tribes used to meet there in the Big Cave, but that was long ago. When the *white-eyes* invaded our lands, we had to leave in a hurry and none of us has been back since the totem brought us to the spirit world.'

Bela reached for Ren-*ya*'s hand. 'I keep thinking I

can hear them, those creatures.' She shuddered. 'What were they?'

'Evil spirits. We call them *sappers*.' Ren-*ya* squeezed her hand. 'Do not worry. They live in underground burrows, never in caves.'

'How did you manage to get me out?'

'I traded you.'

'For what?'

Ren-*ya* hesitated. 'The *smoke*.'

Bela looked at her in horror. 'But you need it –'

Ren-*ya* cut in. 'I need my sister more.'

Ren-*ya* built up the fire and they shared a meal of cured meat and berry cake.

'There is not much food left,' she said. 'It will be light soon and I will go hunting, but first I have a gift for you.' She reached into her pack and handed something to Bela.

'What is it?'

'A knife.'

Bela pulled the stone blade from its rawhide sheath and tested the keen edge against her thumb. She examined it carefully. The blade was fitted into a handle that was smooth and pale, almost white. 'Is it wood?'

Ren-*ya* shook her head. 'Whalebone.'

Bela turned it over in her hand. A design had been scratched into the handle and the marks filled with something black, soot from the fire perhaps. It showed a hunter in a kayak, her harpoon raised above her head. The huge tail of a whale emerged from the surf. The drawing was rough, but she could taste the fierce intent of the hunter, the fright of the prey.

'Did you make it?' she asked.

Ren-*ya* shook her head. 'Mam.'

Bela tried to put the knife back into Ren-*ya*'s hand. 'If Mam gave it to you, you should keep it.'

Ren-*ya* smiled to hear Bela use the familiar name. 'No,' she said. 'I have other things of hers. You have nothing. I want you to have it.'

Bela sighed. 'I wish I could remember her.'

'Do you not remember anything?'

'Maybe,' Bela said. 'There's a certain flavour in this world, something like the taste of sunlight on skin, that I think I've always known.'

Ren-*ya* took Bela's hand. 'She is in your flesh, your blood and your bones. She will always be with you.'

Bela turned back to the gift and traced the outline of the hunter with her fingertip.

Ren-*ya* smiled. 'I am thinking about the time Mam gave it to me. I was crying over my first kill and she was trying to cheer me up.'

Bela looked up at her. 'You cried? Really?'

Ren-*ya* smiled awkwardly. 'Well, yes, but I was only

little then.' She closed her eyes, as if remembering what happened. 'Mam said my feelings were good, that they would stop me being cruel, keep me from killing for its own sake . . . Mam did not mock my tears, but she helped me understand the truth.'

Bela looked up at her. 'The truth?'

'Without death we cannot live.'

Bela thought about the way Ren-*ya* survived, and what she said *was* true. But her mind went back to the mammoth stampede and the professor's men. They died because of what she and Ren-*ya* had done. Bela was sorry for it, but Ren-*ya* was right: they'd had no choice, not if they wanted to live. 'I understand,' she said. 'We'll have to fight for our survival, won't we?'

Ren-*ya* nodded once emphatically. 'Yes, and we must do whatever needs to be done. We will do it with dry eyes or with tears, but whatever happens we will find *Viktonovak* and avenge our mother.' Ren-*ya* closed her hand round Bela's, the one that held the knife. 'We will do it together, as sisters.'

THE DOG-SOLDIER,
THE CAPTAIN AND BLUE-EYE

The embers of the fire were still glowing when Ren-*ya* woke. She put more wood on the fire and ate her breakfast in the warming light.

Her fingers instinctively went to the pocket where she kept the *smoke*, but of course the pouch was gone now. However painful its absence, Ren-*ya* didn't regret it. *Anyone can make a promise,* Mam used to say, *but it is the ones we keep that make us who we are.*

She collected her bow and quiver and headed off.

At the entrance to the caves, the temperature dropped. Ren-*ya* pulled her hood up and stepped out into the frozen dawn. She breathed in and felt the cold pain of it in her lungs, the sting of bitter frost on her face. She sat on a rock and looked down into the valley.

Thick white fog blanketed the forest and only the tops of the tallest trees broke through the mist.

Ren-*ya* let out a cloud of smoky breath into the freezing air. Time to go.

She scrambled over the rocky slopes to the edge of the forest. It had snowed heavily overnight. The trees were furred in pristine white coats and the tracks she'd left the day before were gone. Fog filled the silent spaces between the trees and the only sound in the deadening whiteness was the squeak and crunch of her boots.

It wasn't long before she came across signs of life. Nothing out of the ordinary, just the hoofprints of an elk. She followed them through the forest, hoping to make a quick kill. For a while, the tracks were evenly spaced, but then they veered off, deepened, spaced out. The elk had been running for its life. A little further and Ren-*ya* found what it was fleeing from. A new set of tracks joined the elk's, coming in from the east. They looked like the pawprints of wolves, but smaller. She got down on her knees and sniffed at the mildewy taste of dog.

Ren-*ya* followed the tracks, stopping every few minutes to listen and test the air. But the forest was silent and, other than the taste of dog, the only flavour on her tongue was snow.

After an hour, she came to a thicket where the dogs

had made their kill. There was fresh blood spattered around and a deep, bloodied trench in the snow where the elk's body had been dragged away.

Ren-*ya* licked her lips. The taste of willow sap hung in the air. She followed the drag marks out of the thicket and squatted down by a new set of tracks. With the edge of her glove, she traced the outline of the ridged bootprints.

White-eyes. Two of them.

Ren-*ya*'s blood flowed hot in her veins – maybe *Viktonovak*'s camp was nearby. She got up and hurried after the trail.

By midday, the wind had picked up and cleared the fog away. Ren-*ya* had no choice but to travel into the face of the breeze, so the first she knew of the camp was not the mildewy flavour of the dogs, but the sound of their baying in the distance. She went on cautiously and now she could hear, mingled in with the barking, the sounds of men's voices. She crept forwards and, laying her bow on the ground, squatted down behind the dwindling trees to watch.

The camp was in a clearing at the bottom of a steep ridge. Two ragged *white-eye* men had strung up the body of the elk and were butchering it clumsily. They'd built a ramshackle wooden shelter, and, next to it, an enclosure in which the dogs were penned.

Together, the *white-eyes* carried a sack of elk meat over to the enclosure and threw the steaming chunks to the animals. When they'd emptied the sack, they stood, hands on hips, watching as the beasts pounced on the meat, snarling and snapping over the best pieces. Then they made their way to the shelter, stamped the snow from their boots and went inside.

Ren-*ya* was disappointed. None of these *white-eyes* looked like a leader. *Viktonovak* was not here.

The sound of snapping wood brought Ren-*ya* back to the present and she realized her mistake – her face was to the wind and she had not tasted the approach of another hunter.

She went for her bow, but was too late. A heavy boot stamped on her hand, crushing her fingers. A blow to the back of the neck sent Ren-*ya* sprawling face first into the snow. She lay there, stunned, trying to get her breath. Her hand was released and she cradled it against her chest. Her bow was kicked out of reach.

'Get up,' said a whispered voice behind her. 'Slowly, mind. Don't be doin' nothin' quick.'

Ren-*ya* staggered to her feet.

' 'Ands behind yer back.'

Ren-*ya* put her arms out behind her. They were pulled roughly together and tied tight with a strap that bit deep into her flesh.

'Now, let's be 'avin' a look at yer.'

Ren-*ya*'s attacker pulled her round to face him and yanked the fur hood from her head. He was even more ragged and filthy than the other two *white-eyes*. Unlike them, he was dressed, head to foot, in the black-and-white skins of the dogs. The dog-soldier struggled to draw breath. 'Not much more'n a scrap of a girl,' he choked out.

He brought his face up close to Ren-*ya*'s and his cracked lips opened in a broken-toothed smile. Without warning, he grabbed her by the shoulders and pulled her sharply forward, bringing his knee up hard into her stomach.

Even if she'd known what was coming, Ren-*ya*'s hands were tied and there was no way to defend herself. She fell forward into the snow, curled herself into a ball and coughed her guts up.

The dog-soldier loomed over her. 'Quiet now, black eyes, quiet now.' He got hold of Ren-*ya*'s hair and dragged her towards the wooden shelter at the bottom of the slope.

'What's your name, girl? Where've you come from?'

The man sighed and looked over at the dog-soldier and the other *white-eye*, who warmed themselves in front of the fire.

Ren-*ya* worked a splinter of tooth to the front of her mouth and gobbed it out on to the floor. The dog-soldier had dragged her into the shelter and tied her to a strange wooden structure, what the *white-eyes* called a 'chair'. They'd been firing questions at her for hours, but she hadn't said a word. She tested the strength of the leather strap that kept her hands tied behind her. There was no give in it.

Ren-*ya*'s interrogator grabbed her by the hair, tipped back the chair and yanked her head up. The *white-eye* seemed half-starved and there was no colour in his bloodless face. It was not clear to Ren-*ya* what he was called. The dog-soldier referred to him slyly as 'Lev', but this made him fly into a rage, and insist his name was 'Captain'.

He glanced over at the others. 'Look at those weird black eyes. Gives me the creeps.'

One of the men looked up. His face was covered in bruises and one eye was swollen shut, as if he'd been in a fight. The other eye, which seemed to see right through Ren-*ya*, was deep sky-blue. 'She doesn't say much, does she?'

The captain tightened his grip on Ren-*ya*'s hair. 'You try making it bleat then.' Flecks of spit flew from between his teeth and the peppery stench of sickness on his breath turned Ren-*ya*'s stomach.

Blue-eye held up his hand. 'I only meant maybe it doesn't speak . . . but I'll have a go if you insist.'

He made to get up from his seat, but the dog-soldier grabbed him by the arm. 'Why not chop 'er up, feed 'er to the dogs?' He drew in a noisy lungful of air. 'Save us huntin' fer a few days.'

Blue-eye shook him off. 'You know our orders. We find anything, we take it to the professor.'

'Orders?' said the dog-soldier, rolling his eyes. 'Why should we do anythin' he says? He's left us to die out 'ere. Look at the state of us. I could *breathe* before I came 'ere. Every day goes by, we gets worse.' As if to prove his point, he ended in a fit of coughing.

Ren-*ya* pricked up her ears at this. The peppery taste of sickness seeped from the pores of all three *white-eyes* and her heart leaped as she understood the cause: their presence in the spirit world was making them ill.

The dog-soldier continued with his complaints. 'He tricked us, lured us to that estate of his with talk of riches and power. He said we could go back 'ome whenever we wanted, but he's a liar –'

Suddenly the captain launched himself at the dog-soldier, grabbing him round the neck. 'Have you no decency, no loyalty?' He kept a tight hold as the dog-soldier clawed at his hands, gasping for breath.

'That's enough,' Blue-eye said mildly. 'Let him be.'

But the captain didn't let go, and the dog-soldier began to choke.

'You'll kill him,' Blue-eye said, although he sounded as if he didn't much care one way or the other.

At last the captain released him and kicked the dog-soldier's chair over, sending him sprawling on to the floor.

He turned to Blue-eye. 'So we're agreed? We'll

start out tomorrow, take her to the professor.'

Blue-eye rubbed his chin. 'It's a long way to go. Two days' march. And those dogs are always hungry.'

'Yes, but what if she turns out to be important?'

Blue-eye looked at Ren-*ya* and narrowed his eyes. 'Well, all right then.' He nodded towards the dog-soldier who was still gasping for breath. 'What about him?'

'He can stay here and look after the dogs.'

After that, they left Ren-*ya* alone. The dog-soldier, once he'd recovered, prepared a meal, turning a haunch of venison on a spit over the fire. Ren-*ya* hung her head and closed her eyes, but she listened to every word the *white-eyes* said. She learned they were part of a larger group garrisoned many miles away, under the command of the man she was seeking. Each of them had committed some small crime and been banished to this backwater as a punishment. The captain and Blue-eye had been officers and felt their punishment more keenly than the dog-soldier, who was only a carpenter, they said. Even so, it was the dog-soldier who did most of the complaining.

'He said we'd be like kings,' he muttered to himself as he turned the meat. 'But are we? No, we're stuck 'ere in this stinkin' hut at the edge of the world.'

The sun went down and darkness fell. The three *white-eyes* ate the venison and settled down in front of the fire, scratching at the lice in their furs.

'This could be our chance,' the captain said to Blue-eye. 'We could be back in favour, reinstated as officers.'

The dog-soldier made a breathy, gasping noise and Ren-*ya* thought he was choking again, but it seemed he was laughing. 'Quit yer dreamin'. He don't forgive nothin' or nobody.'

BLUE-EYE AND THE BIRD

Ren-*ya* didn't sleep. Partly it was the throbbing pain of her injuries, the numbness of her wrists and hands. That and hunger and thirst. Then there was the snoring of the three *white-eyes*. The dog-soldier was laid out on the floor on his back, and all night his breath bubbled in and out of his lungs. Ren-*ya* spent the sleepless hours thinking how stupid she'd been, allowing herself to get caught.

But these weren't the thoughts that troubled her the most. Ren-*ya* had said she wouldn't leave Bela, whatever happened. It cut her to the bone that her sister would think she'd broken her promise. It left her with a sickness in her stomach like grief.

In the morning, Blue-eye gave Ren-*ya* water and

cold venison, greasy with congealed fat. Her mouth was swollen and she had a hard time chewing and swallowing, but she forced it down. They'd be out in the forest for at least two days, and Ren-*ya* would need her strength if she was going to have any chance of escape.

When it was time to go, the captain cut the leather strap binding her hands and dragged her to her feet. He watched as Ren-*ya* rubbed the blood back into her fingers. He held up two circles joined together with a strap. It was all made of some coldly shining stuff that Ren-*ya* had never seen before. 'You won't be running off anywhere when I've got these shackles on you,' he said with a sly smile.

He kneeled down and snapped the hoops shut round Ren-*ya*'s ankles. 'And I'm the one with the key,' he said, dropping a small glinting instrument into his pocket.

Ren-*ya* took an experimental step. The strap was just long enough so she could walk, but too short to run.

The captain watched her, no doubt hoping to get some pleasure out of her discomfort. He drew a blade from its sheath and held it against Ren-*ya*'s cheek. 'Cross me, and first chance I get I'll mess that pretty face up some more.' He gave her a shove and Ren-*ya* staggered back. The strap went taut and she fell heavily to the ground.

Blue-eye looked up from pulling on his boots. 'Get her up – it's time to go.'

The captain pulled Ren-*ya* to her feet, shoved her through the open door and out into the forest.

The temperature had dropped overnight and it felt too cold even for snow. As soon as the air hit her skin, Ren-*ya*'s eyes started streaming and she wiped the tears away before they could freeze on her face.

Blue-eye led the way, setting a brisk pace, and it was hard to keep up with the shackles on. Each time she fell behind, the captain gave her a hard shove between the shoulder blades.

For the first hour, Blue-eye and the captain kept up a banter between them, fantasizing about what they would do, what they would eat and drink when they got back to what they called 'civilization'. But as the cold bit deep, they fell silent.

Walking was an agony for Ren-*ya*. Even through her boots, the shackles rubbed the skin from her ankles with every step, although after a while the cold seeped into her feet and the pain subsided to numbness.

By midday, the wind had picked up. They trudged on, heads bowed, each of them an island of freezing misery. Ren-*ya* was so cold and tired she couldn't think straight and the hours passed in a blur. For seconds or minutes at a time, she seemed to lose consciousness.

She would come back to herself and the bitter cold with a lurch, surprised to find she was still upright, still putting one heavy foot in front of the other. During one of those blank moments she must've slowed her pace, because suddenly she felt a thud between her shoulder blades and she was flat out in the snow.

Ren-*ya* heard the captain snarl, 'Get up.'

She tried to get on to her knees, but was too weak. She lay back on the ground. All she wanted to do was lie there and sleep.

'I said, get up.'

An agonizing spasm in her ribs made Ren-*ya* curl into a ball.

Then Blue-eye's voice. 'Leave her – she's had enough. We need her alive. Help me get her up.'

They got hold of Ren-*ya*'s arms and dragged her up against the trunk of a tree. Blue-eye held a water bottle to her lips and she drank, only she was shaking so much that most of it dribbled out of her mouth again.

'Eat.' Blue-eye held a piece of dried meat under her nose. The smell turned Ren-*ya*'s stomach and she coughed the water back up. The white glare off the snow set off a sick thudding in her head and she shut her eyes.

'She's in a bad way,' Blue-eye said. 'We should've waited till she was stronger.'

'Nah, she's putting it on.'

'She's not going to make it like this. Give me the key.'

'Are you joking?'

'Come off it,' Blue-eye said. 'Look at her – she's a mess. She's not going anywhere.'

Ren-*ya* heard the click as the shackles were unlocked. 'You idiot!' Blue-eye said. 'You put them on too tight. If she can't walk, *I'm* not going to be the one who carries her.'

There was a raw band of weeping flesh around each of Ren-*ya*'s ankles and Blue-eye bandaged them with strips of hide. After that, Ren-*ya* was allowed to walk at her own pace, without the captain shoving her in the back. They gave her food and water and stopped from time to time to let her rest. She was in a lot of pain, but now the shackles were off she began to regain her strength. Even so, Ren-*ya* acted up, putting in the odd stumble every now and again, as if she was exhausted and ill, hoping it would be enough to give her an edge. Her act seemed to convince Blue-eye, but the captain wasn't taken in so easily. When they stopped, Blue-eye fussed about, feeding Ren-*ya* bits of dried meat and holding the water bottle to her lips as she drank. But the captain stood apart, arms folded, shaking his head.

Late in the afternoon, they stopped in a clearing for another break. Ren-*ya* was chewing on a piece of the

foul dried meat when the captain looked
up. 'It's that black-and-white bird again.
I reckon it's following us.'

'Don't be stupid,' Blue-eye said. 'They
all look the same.'

But Ren-*ya* knew he was wrong. She waited
until the soldiers weren't looking and threw a
piece of dried meat into the snow. The magpie
flicked its tail and flew down silently to retrieve it.
The bird looked at Ren-*ya* for a
long moment, its head on one side,
before flying back into the trees.

The captain stood up and stretched. 'I'm off for a minute – call of nature.' He nodded towards Ren-*ya*. 'Don't be fooled by that one. Keep your eye on her,' he said as he went off into the trees.

Ren-*ya*'s heart kicked up a beat. This could be her chance. She started rubbing her legs and staggered to her feet as if she needed to stretch them.

But Blue-eye was no fool. 'Sit down! I'll have those shackles on quick as a flash if you try anything funny.'

Ren-*ya* squatted back down in the snow. Only now, Blue-eye was suspicious. He was so intent on Ren-*ya* that he didn't notice the bird had returned and was perched on a low-hanging branch just behind him.

The magpie cocked its head. Its look seemed to say, *Are you ready for this?*

But Ren-*ya* could never have guessed what was coming next.

The bird took off, swooped down and scratched at Blue-eye's head with its claws. The soldier was taken by surprise. He tried to bat the bird away with his hands, but when he turned his face up to see what was attacking him, the magpie took its chance. In one supple movement, the bird dipped its head and stabbed at the soldier's upturned face. It tore out his blue eye with its long black beak and carried it away into the trees.

Blue-eye plunged around blindly, shouting and clutching his face. Ren-*ya* was rooted to the spot by the sight of his face, running with blood. It wasn't until she heard the captain crashing back through the undergrowth that she began to think clearly again and started to run.

But the deprivations of the journey had taken their toll and Ren-*ya* was slow. She looked back and there was the captain, rushing back into the clearing, his face a picture of shock.

As Ren-*ya* ran, she heard the sound of Blue-eye's screams and her own ragged breath in the freezing air.

Suddenly there was a deafening crack and Ren-*ya* was stopped dead by an agonizing pain in the back of her leg. She took another few staggering steps, struggling to stay upright, to hold on to consciousness, but it slipped away and she fell into darkness, face down in the snow.

TWO VOICES IN THE DARK

The fire had almost burned out when Bela woke, and she hurried to light the hurricane lamp from Ren-*ya*'s pack. The yellow flame rose up and in its flickering glow she saw the fur Ren-*ya* had slept in was lying on the rock floor, empty.

Bela forced down a breakfast of cold meat and pine nuts, but the food didn't stop the biting unease in the pit of her stomach. *Ren-ya will be back soon*, she told herself. There was nothing here to be afraid of.

She drank the last of the water and went through to the Big Cave to look for more. She held up the lamp. Stalagmites like marble pillars rose from the floor of the cave and disappeared into the inky blackness above her head. A creeping dread made her shiver. The cavern was so huge that the rays of her lamp didn't reach the walls. She was alone in the middle of a tiny bubble of light, a weak, flickering defence against the vast darkness that surrounded her.

She went on, sticking close to the edge of the cavern. The light of her lamp crawled up the walls, revealing the many colours of the different minerals. Here and there the rock was damp and encrusted with salt crystals. A seam of gold was sandwiched between variegated greens and blues and she followed it to an overhanging rock where clusters of stalactites dripped water into a pool below. Bela wondered if these caves still existed in the waking world or whether they'd been buried under ice sheets or blocked by rockfalls. She had never seen anything like them and realized she must be one of the few people who ever would. She kneeled down and filled the water skin, scooped the icy water up in her hands and splashed it on her face.

There was a low rumbling like the sound of heavy furniture scraping across a floor. Bela stopped dead. Was it Ren-*ya* coming back? She stayed still and listened, but there was nothing now except the dripping of water. The seconds blinked by, but the caves remained silent. Did she imagine it? Or was it only the echo of moving water? She wiped her face on her sleeve and steadied her breathing, telling herself she was too old to still be afraid of the dark.

Even so, the feeling of being trapped inside the rock was fraying her nerves and she decided to find the way out and wait for Ren-*ya* where she could at least see daylight.

She got up and peered into the darkness. Ren-*ya* had said there were many tunnels and caverns leading off the Big Cave. Bela decided to follow the cave wall – in the end, she was bound to come to the tunnel that led to the entrance.

She began to skirt round the edge of the cave and it wasn't long before she came to the opening of a tunnel. Here salt crystals grew on every surface and her light was reflected back at her in a rainbow of colours.

She made her way along the tunnel until it divided into two. Only one could lead to the entrance; the other might go deeper into the heart of the mountain. Ren-*ya*'s warning came back to her: *Do not go wandering. Those tunnels are a labyrinth.* Bela would have to remember the turnings so she didn't get lost.

She took the left fork into a bare grey corridor of rock, but she'd only gone a few feet when the tunnel split in two again. She was about to turn back when a pungent flavour stopped her in her tracks. Bela lifted her lamp. In the trembling light, she saw the shape of a human hand on the wall. It was outlined in a fine ochre-coloured mist that splayed out from each of the fingers. She'd seen something similar in her father's journals: ancient cave paintings made by the ancestors of humans. It was devastating to think how much he would have loved to be there, how much he'd not lived to see.

Further along, she spotted another painted hand, and another. There were paintings of animals too. Bela recognized the spotted coats of hyenas, the heads of bison and bears. As she moved down the tunnel, she found the outline of a cave lion drawn on the rock with ochre and soot. The painted hands were clustered round this drawing like a shrine. She drew in a deep breath. She could sense that something terrible had happened here. The paintings must have been made thousands of years ago, yet the tormented flavour of dust the artist had left behind was still painfully fresh.

The further Bela went into the labyrinth, the more hands appeared. They were painted in a chaotic frenzy, one on top of another, like the leaves of trees in a great forest. As the lamplight jumped and flickered on the walls, it set the painted hands in motion; the canopy of outstretched fingers seemed to be reaching out of the darkness, searching for the light.

Bela followed the painted hands down more turns and branches of the tunnel. There was another taste here, something earthy, mineral. She wondered if it was the lingering flavour of the ochre paint, but it seemed impossible after thousands of years. She reached out to touch the reddish pigment. To her surprise, it was damp and came off on her fingers.

Her stomach turned. The marks were freshly painted.

Bela was trying to work out what this could mean when she heard the rumbling sound again. This time it came to her clearly. The sound drew itself out, ending in a note of despair like the deep bellow of a tortured creature.

Bela stood frozen, hardly daring to breathe as it echoed through the caverns. This time she knew it wasn't Ren-*ya* returning. There was something in here with her, lurking out of sight in the dark corridors of rock.

Bela's instinct told her to run. But in which direction? She didn't know where the sound was coming from, but the thought of losing herself in the labyrinth of tunnels made her mind up for her and she began to creep back towards the Big Cave. At each turn in the tunnel, she stopped and listened. All she could hear now was her own heartbeat thudding in her ears like a giant's footsteps.

She was nearing the Big Cave when she turned a corner and saw a light flickering on the rock at the far end of the tunnel. She stumbled back and tried to shield the light of her own lamp. But she was too late.

'There's someone in here with us, Nort.' The voice had a wheedling urgency that burrowed into her mind. 'Go and see, Nort. Go and see.'

Bela turned and ran. Close behind her, the voice echoed in the tunnels. 'Find it, Nort! Catch it!'

She ran headlong into the heart of the mountain, into the labyrinth of dividing tunnels, hardly noticing which way she went as she stumbled on, her lungs bursting. Behind her, the footsteps of her pursuers clashed on the rocks, but she was faster and the sly voice got fainter as she hurtled on through the darkness.

Suddenly she burst out of the network of tunnels into a flat-roofed cavern and stood swaying on the lip of a swirling eddy of dark water that filled the cave. She recognized the whirlpool from Ren-*ya*'s description. *The way ahead was underwater* – she couldn't go any further. She'd run herself into a dead end.

From the labyrinth behind her, Bela could hear them coming. She held the lamp up high, looking for somewhere, anywhere, to hide. To one side, there was a narrow ledge that skirted the whirlpool. She climbed up and pressed her back to the rock wall. Feeling the way ahead with one hand, she took a shaking step away from the entrance. After a few steps, she came to a shallow depression in the rock behind her. She pressed her body into the narrow alcove, hoping it would be deep enough to hide her.

She lifted the glass on the hurricane lamp and drew a breath to blow it out. She hesitated – the flickering flame was like her own life, her beating heart. It was her only hope of finding the way out, but whatever was coming for her was more frightening than being lost in the dark. She blew the flame out.

Now the only light was the faint glow cast by the mouth of the cave, shining on the opposite wall. As the footsteps approached, it brightened, glinting on the shining minerals embedded in the rock. Bela held her breath. She tried to make herself disappear into the face of the rock.

A dark silhouette moved into the light, the murky

shadow of a massive head on immense shoulders. The shadow crept up the wall, monstrous and huge, until it filled the cave and blocked out the light. The creature was hunched over, too big to stand in the low-roofed cavern. All she could make out in the gloom was its hand, strangely pale, naked and human, clutching a burning pine branch that spat tiny sparks on to the rocky floor.

Then the creature came forward into the light. It had the shape of a man, but its body was covered in fur and it had the head of a cave lion on its massive shoulders. The monster that had pursued her was just like the stone carving she'd seen in her father's study, what seemed now like a lifetime ago.

The creature sniffed the air, probed the darkness for her as it swung its massive head from side to side. Its gaze swept round like a searchlight to the ledge where she was hidden. She shrank back into the alcove and swallowed down the sick fear that rose up to choke her. Her mind refused to believe it was real and she told herself it must be a shaman wearing a mask. But when the creature spoke, the sound it made was deep and terrible and unlike any human voice she'd heard before. 'Where are you hiding? Show yourself.'

And then that other wheedling voice: 'You've lost it in the tunnels, you fool.'

The creature bellowed in reply. Its huge shadow writhed on the wall and the choking taste of dust filled Bela's mouth. The roar of the beast was full of unbearable pain. It seemed to echo in her flesh, long after his cries had faded away and the only sound that remained was the sucking black water at her feet. The monster's dark silhouette turned and began to move away. For a few seconds, his receding shadow played on the wall, and then it disappeared, leaving behind only the dusty taste of its torment on Bela's tongue.

For a long time, she stayed where she was, clinging to the ledge, too afraid to move. She didn't know how much time went by – enough to get her breath back and for her leaping heartbeat to slow.

Time had passed strangely when she was caught in the *sappers'* trap and she remembered how the walls of the tunnel had clutched her like a straightjacket of frozen earth. Now the darkness held her just as close. She wanted to scream, but if she opened her mouth the dark would creep in, get inside her. She mustn't make a sound. She must be as silent as the dead.

She reminded herself that Ren-*ya* would be back soon and at first she felt a surge of hope, but then she imagined her returning, finding Bela gone, calling her name. In her mind's eye, Bela saw the beast prick up its ears, and the other sly-voiced creature urging its companion to catch this new intruder. She had to get out and warn Ren-*ya* before it was too late.

Every journey begins with a first small step. Slowly, Bela slid her foot along to the left. Carefully, she dragged her other foot across to meet it. Already her heart was galloping in her chest. The feeling of empty space around her made her dizzy and she grabbed at the wall to steady herself, her useless lamp clattering against the rock.

Frustration made her want to cry out, but she waited until her balance returned and started again. One faltering step at a time until her hand fumbled into empty space and she knew she'd found the entrance to the cave.

She stepped down from the ledge and stood, listening. All she could hear was her own ragged breathing and the movement of that great black body of water. She started down the tunnel, feeling her way with her hands, shuffling her feet forward inch by inch. After a few minutes, she came to a fork. She thought back, tried to recreate the memory, but all that came to her was the feeling of fear that had kept her running blind, not caring which way she went. She remembered turning many corners, her little pool of light jerking and swinging.

It was hopeless. Even if she could see where she was going, she'd be lost.

But it wouldn't help to think like that. Bela told herself to be brave, to stop coming up with reasons why she'd fail. *You've got to trust yourself*, she thought. *Trust your instinct*. After all, it was the only thing she had left to guide her.

She stopped trying to use logic to work out which way to go. Instead, if her gut told her to go left, she did. When the way ahead branched, she hardly hesitated. She just kept going, inching forward in the direction that felt right.

She continued on like this, edging her way along the network of tunnels for what seemed like hours. She'd just started to think she must have gone the wrong way when she caught a flavour on the air and her heart leaped. It was faint but unmistakable: the taste of the ochre pigment. She must be close to the tunnel with the painted hands.

Sniffing at the air like a dog, she carried on. She would lose the scent for desperate minutes before hope kicked in when she picked it up again. The further she went, the stronger the taste. She felt along the walls until her fingers stumbled on a damp patch of rock. She rubbed her fingertips together, lifted them to her face and tasted the ochre pigment that had been used to paint the hands.

An image of the lion-man came into her head. She pictured his strange human hands and a shiver took hold of her. The choking taste in her mouth was the same as his tortured cry. It was him; he'd made the marks that crawled across the rock, yearning for the light.

Bela continued on more quickly now, desperate to escape. As she turned into the last tunnel, the air cooled. She could hear the sound of dripping water and her breathing quickened as she groped her way along, with the sharp salt crystals grazing her fingertips. She was nearly there.

Suddenly she tipped into space and fell. Her body hit hard rock and she cried out. The sound was deafening as her scream echoed back at her from every direction.

As her cry faded, it was answered by a deep, rumbling roar, as if the mountain, or her head, had split open.

NORT

When Bela came to, her head was pounding.

She had a vague sense of having been lifted up, of having been carried to the place where she now lay. She opened her eyes as wide as they would go, but could see nothing, only thick black darkness. The smell of pine needles drifted in the air, and beneath that a taste that was neither human nor beast. She could hear a faint sound nearby, the long, slow breaths of sleep.

Suddenly a harsh voice cut through the dark. 'Wake up, Nort.'

Bela lay completely still and listened. She heard the lion-man sigh deep in his throat.

'Wake up, I said!'

This time, the monster spoke. 'Can't you leave me

alone for once? I'm tired. Let me sleep.'

'You've slept enough. There's things to be done.'

'Leave me alone, Tron, or I will pull you limb from limb.'

The other creature laughed. 'And how would you do that? You know very well you can't live without me. *I* am the master here.'

Bela's heart seemed to shrink inside her. She'd glimpsed the lion-man's hideous form, but the unseen voice in the darkness frightened her more.

Tron's voice set off again. 'Nort . . .? Are you listening? Do you remember what happened last time you tried to defy me?'

'I don't remember anything,' Nort replied, although the tremor in his voice told Bela he knew exactly what Tron was talking about.

Tron sniggered. 'Shall I remind you?'

'Please . . . don't . . .'

'Do you remember how I tore you apart in the darkness, how I cut you in two?' The creature spoke softly now, lingering on every word as if he was enjoying it. 'Do you remember how I *unravelled* you?' Tron giggled. 'I remember how you twisted and turned, Nort. You tried to get away, but you couldn't, could you?'

The lion-man groaned pitifully and Bela curled herself up into a ball. She pressed her hands to her ears, but Tron's insinuating voice crept in.

'I was always someone who enjoyed his work. I can see them now; can *you*? All those shiny instruments laid out in a row. You can tell that somebody has spared no effort to polish them up. Now which one shall I choose? Why don't you help me decide, Nort? Which one would you say looks the nastiest? Which one can't you stop yourself looking at?' He let this vile thought hang in the air before he was off again. 'I know! I know exactly what you're thinking! I have the same problem myself. They're all horrible, aren't they? And it makes it very hard to decide which one is going to hurt you the most.'

He paused for a moment, and although Bela fought it, in her head she couldn't help seeing a row of shiny instruments to which her imagination added points and hooks and blades. The image took her back to the professor's laboratory and the cruelties she had seen there.

'Well, let me tell you a secret, Nort . . . They're *all* going to hurt you!' Tron laughed as if this was the funniest joke, but then his voice dropped and he became deadly serious. 'I'm going to rub you out. You'll be nothing, Nort, nobody.'

Bela couldn't stand it any longer. 'Shut up!' she shouted. 'Leave him alone!'

Tron's voice stopped dead. There was a scuffling

noise, a movement in the air around her, and then the only sound remaining was the panting distress of the lion-man.

What had she done? She'd acted on impulse and had no idea what to do next. She pictured the creature's dreadful head sweeping from side to side as he searched for her in the darkness.

After a while, Nort's breathing slowed. 'He's gone,' he said.

'Where?' Her voice shook as she wondered where Tron was hiding, what he planned to do next.

'I don't know where he goes, but he'll be back.' The lion-man shifted about in the dark. 'Why did you stand up for me? Aren't you afraid?'

'You chased me.'

'No, you ran away. This is *my* home.'

'Then I'll leave. Just show me the way out.'

'And have you tell my enemies where I am? Who sent you?'

Bela had no idea what enemies such a creature would have, but she knew she had to show him she could be trusted. 'No one sent me,' she said.

'Then why are you here?'

Bela hesitated. She thought about telling the truth, but the creature was already suspicious and if he knew she wasn't alone it might convince him she was an enemy. 'I can't speak to you like this in the dark,' she said. 'Please . . . will you light a lamp?'

'I have no lamp and no need of one,' he snapped. And then, more quietly, 'I don't want you to see me.'

'I already have. I was hiding in the cave with the whirlpool.'

'Then you know why I prefer the dark.'

They didn't speak for a moment and Bela listened anxiously for Tron's return, but the silence of the caves was as deep as the darkness.

'Why does he say those things to you?' she said.

'He enjoys it. He likes to make my life a misery.'

'Then why don't you leave?'

There was a long silence before he replied. 'I can never leave. My enemies are out there.'

'You could fight him then.'

'He's too strong.'

Bela found this hard to believe. She'd seen the lion-man, his vast size, and it seemed impossible Tron could be stronger. 'What kind of creature is he?' she asked.

'I've never seen him. I live in the dark, and whenever I light a torch he stays behind me. When I turn round, he slips away. I hear him though. I hear his voice and it tortures me.'

There was something pitiable about Nort. Despite his strength and power, he let himself be terrorized, and he hid in the dark, too afraid to go outside.

'Does Tron mean me any harm?' Bela asked. Nort was silent and a cold shudder ran through her.

At last he spoke. 'He tells me you're a spy.'

'I promise you, I'm not.'

'Then tell me why you're here.'

'If I do, will you let me go? Will you show me the way out?'

Nort grunted. 'Let's hear your story first, and then we'll see.'

Bela told him about her mother and father, about the professor and how she came to be here.

When she'd finished, Nort said, 'So there's another world, different to this one?'

'Didn't you know?'

'Maybe I did once, but I've long forgotten.'

'Where do *you* come from then?'

'I'm not sure,' he said. 'But I believe . . . I *know* that I've not always been as I am now.'

'What do you mean?'

'I've not always been a beast. Once I was human. I'm sure of it.'

'Because of your hands?'

'Not only that. If this was my natural state, I wouldn't be ashamed. I wouldn't need to hide in the dark.'

'There's no need to feel ashamed for what you can't help,' Bela said. 'Light your torch and let me see.'

There was a spark and then the torch the creature held jumped to life. He sat, head hanging down, hunched up on a bed of pine branches. His huge shoulders were pressed against the low roof of the cave. She'd known what to expect, but up close he seemed bigger, more terrible, and she couldn't suppress a shudder of horror.

Slowly, he raised his head and his dark shadow rose with it to fill the cave. He looked right at her, and Bela forced herself not to flinch, not to turn away. She made herself look back into his shining amber eyes.

'What is your name?' he said.

'Bela.'

He nodded his ugly head. 'Bela.' He said it reverently, as if it was a precious thing. 'Your story has touched what little heart I have. In return, I will show you the way out, but I'm tired now and I must sleep.'

He put the pine-branch torch down on the cave floor and stamped on it.

'Please,' she said. 'Don't leave me in the dark.'

He held out the smouldering wood and she crept forward and lit her lamp.

TRON

Bela watched as Nort curled up like a child. She knew she had little choice but to trust him and hope that, when he woke up, he'd show her the way out of the labyrinth.

When he'd fallen asleep, Bela lifted the lamp and looked around.

There was only one way in and out of the cave. From where she was sitting, she could look down the narrow tunnel that led away. When Tron returned, at least she'd see him coming. She tilted the lamp so its circle of light fell on the beast.

Nort moaned in his sleep and yawned. She caught sight of his teeth, long and sharp at the front of his jaw, the tearing molars at the back. Her gaze flicked to his hands, which were curled under his massive jaw. It was hard to believe he'd been human once. Bela wondered what would happen to him when she left. Tron would continue to torment him, she was sure of that.

She turned these thoughts over in her mind, all the time listening for Ren-*ya*, who should've been back long ago. Listening too for Tron, who was out there somewhere.

When the lamp started to die down, she called Nort's name. He didn't wake, so she got up and stretched out her hand, but she couldn't touch him. It wasn't his ugliness that repelled her. It was nothing to do with how he looked on the outside. It was *him*, and it was pity, not fear, that made her pull her hand away.

She called his name again, louder this time, and he began to stir.

'Wake up,' she said. 'It's time for us to leave this place forever.'

'Us?' he said, rubbing his eyes.

'Come with me, Nort. Leave that creature behind.'

He looked up at her. 'But I'm a monster. Why would you want to help me?'

'Tron is the monster, not you.'

'Without him, I'll die.'

'What if he's lying to you?'

'I'm afraid . . . not of dying, because then my

suffering would be at an end. I'm afraid of *living*, of leaving this place and going out into the light.'

'I'll help you.'

Nort fell silent while hope and despair chased each other across his face. 'Tron will never let me go.'

'He doesn't *own* you. Let's go now, together.' Bela got up, and although her heart was beating hard and her body shook with horror, she held her hand out to him. Tears streamed down his face as he took it.

He lit a torch from Bela's lamp before she blew it out, and they headed off. The tunnel that led away from the cave twisted and turned with many forks in the path, but Nort never faltered. He led the way, crouched over in the narrow space.

Suddenly he stopped. 'Did you hear that?'

Bela strained her ears, but she could hear nothing.

The torch trembled in his hand. 'I thought I heard his voice.'

They went on through the labyrinth until they emerged in the Big Cave. Bela hurried to the small cavern where she and Ren-*ya* had camped, but the blackened ashes of the fire pit were untouched. Everything was exactly as she'd left it.

Tears welled up in her eyes. She'd hoped, *counted* on Ren-*ya* being there.

She turned her face away from Nort and quickly

wiped her eyes. The lion-man was a beast with immeasurable power, yet it was Bela who would have to be strong and lead them out of the mountain.

She turned back to him. 'There's furs and a little dried meat. Let's take as much as we can carry and go . . .'

Nort wasn't listening. He was holding the torch above his head, staring off into the darkness of the cavern.

'What is it?' Bela said. 'What's wrong?'

'He's coming.'

Bela peered into the pitch-black. She could see nothing beyond their small circle of light. 'Where?'

Suddenly Tron's voice cut through the darkness. 'What have we here? Beauty and the beast?'

Bela stepped back, sheltering behind Nort's huge body.

'Don't tell me she's sweet-talked you into believing she's your friend?' Tron sniggered. 'What would a girl like her want with a vile monster like you?'

As he talked, Bela put down the lamp and unsheathed her whalebone knife.

'I warned you, Nort. I told you – she's a spy!'

'Don't listen to him,' Bela whispered. 'I'm not a spy. I *am* your friend.'

Tron giggled. '*She's* a tricky one, and so convincing. She makes you *want* to believe her, doesn't she?'

Nort didn't reply. He only moaned quietly and

began to swing his head from side to side.

Bela tightened her grip on the knife. 'We're leaving, Tron. Don't try to stop us . . . I'm not afraid of you. I'll kill you if I have to.'

'Hear that, Nort? She really is a piece of work.'

Again, the lion-man didn't reply. He seemed to have fallen into a kind of trance.

'After all,' Tron continued, 'what kind of friend would take you away from where you're safe, force you out into the light and expose you to your enemies?'

Bela peered out from behind the bulk of Nort's body. 'Where is he?' she whispered.

The lion-man turned slowly towards her.

'Surely you see what she is now?'

It seemed to be Nort who spoke, but it was Tron's voice that Bela heard. She watched in confusion as the lion-man's face changed. He began to shake and moan. Then, just as quickly, a calculating look crossed his face. 'Finish her, Nort,' he said. 'Kill the girl before she has a chance to betray us.'

It was the lion-man who spat out those vile words and who in turn cringed and cried at hearing them. In that moment, Bela realized that Nort and Tron were one and the same.

'Nort!' Bela tried to shake him from his trance. 'You've got to fight against him!'

The lion-man groaned in agony, but an instant later it was Tron's cruel eyes that looked back at her. It was Tron who took her by the throat, who lifted her from her feet and held her in his monstrous fist.

The knife slipped out of Bela's grasp and fell to the floor.

The beast lifted the torch, and in its light she saw that Nort had gone and Tron's narrowed eyes searched her face. Bela fought him for her life. She kicked and punched with all the strength she had, but she soon ran out of air and hung there, weak and limp in his grasp.

The lion-man lowered his head to hers. His shining eyes reflected her terrified face, her narrow throat encircled by his fist, and around her neck the leather strap and the totem, twisting and sparkling with its swirling pinpricks of light.

Inky darkness gathered at the edge of Bela's vision. A deep silence rolled in around her. She was touching oblivion when the grip round her throat suddenly loosened and she fell to the ground, gasping for breath.

The dark silhouette of the lion-man loomed over her. He stretched his

hand out towards her and she saw him grasp the totem before she squeezed her eyes shut. She felt a sharp tug at her throat and then . . . nothing.

There was a strange noise, a rushing like the wind, the clamour of whispered voices.

Bela opened her eyes, and there was the pine branch, spitting on the floor, its faint light almost extinguished. Beyond it she saw a tangled shape that glowed in the darkness. She couldn't make out what it was. It rose up, shrank back, rose again, before it fell, writhing, to the ground. At last it lay there, dark and still.

Bela staggered to her feet, picked up the pine branch and felt around until she found the hurricane lamp. She lit it with a shaking hand and, by its light, found her whalebone knife.

Holding the blade out in front of her, she crept towards the dark mound that now lay quiet in the gloom. She tasted earth and tarnished metal, that now-familiar taste of ancient power. Bela lifted the lamp, unsure of what she expected to see. Nort perhaps, returned to his better self.

Instead, the body of a human man lay on the floor. He was curled up like a sleeping child, his hands clenched into fists by his head. Next to him, something smouldered and bubbled, licked with tiny flames. She picked it up with the tip of the knife and held it to the light. It was paper-thin and seemed to weigh nothing. Then she realized what it was and dropped it. With a shudder, she kicked it away. It was dried-up skin. When the monster transformed into a man, he must have shed his lion skin, like a snake.

With the knife poised in her fist, she reached out with her boot and nudged him, but he remained completely still. She kneeled down, pressed her hand to his neck. His skin was cold, but his pulse was strong. He was alive.

But who was he? The creature, Nort or Tron, whoever he was, had become a man. Or gone back to being a man. Hadn't he said he was sure he was human once? Bela held the lamp close to his face. His skin was smeared with dirt and his hair and beard were long and matted, but there was something familiar about him. Could he be one of the sleeping men she'd seen in the attic of Wilder House?

She fetched a fur and, as she threw it over him, she noticed something gripped in his hand. The totem.

She remembered the spinning reflection of it in the mirror of Tron's eyes, his hand reaching out, the sharp tug at her throat. It must have been the touch of the totem that had caused his transformation.

Bela kneeled down and roughly prised his fingers open. As she took the shining stone back, he murmured a single word.

She drew back from him, her heart thudding. That word, it might have been *mother*, but then her heart leaped right into her throat. It could have been *Nagar*.

Bela held the totem up and watched as it turned hypnotically on its leather strap. She dragged her gaze back to the man on the floor. What did he want with it?

She shivered. The air was cooler here and she was cold and, she realized, hungry and thirsty. It was a long time since she'd had something to eat, since she'd slept. She got some logs for the fire. They were tinder dry and she soon had a blaze going. She ate the last of the dried meat and a handful of pine nuts.

Afterwards, she wrapped herself in a fur, keeping the fire between her and the man. Her eyes were heavy and the warmth of the flames made her tired, but she knew it would be stupid to let herself fall asleep. She forced her eyes to stay open and propped herself up against the wall with the whalebone knife in her lap.

VIKTONOVAK'S PRISONER

When Ren-*ya* came to, she found herself lying on a raised wooden platform. She struggled up on to her elbows, wincing at a throbbing pain in her leg.

She was inside a shelter of some kind. The only light came from a hurricane lamp on a table at the far side of the room. A man dressed in a fur coat was hunched over it, humming to himself. He turned and, seeing Ren-*ya* was awake, brought the lamp over and put it down beside her. 'Know where you are?' he said.

Ren-*ya* shook her head.

'This whole place is under the command of Viktor Novak.' He swept an arm round the room. 'This is the infirmary.'

'Infirmary?'

'A place where the sick are made well again.'

Ren-*ya*'s gaze darted about. She noted the heavy door, the tiny barred window high up in the wall. Escape wouldn't be easy. It was more like a prison than a sickroom.

The man laughed softly. 'I can see you're keen to be out of here, but that all depends on the professor's orders.'

'What will he do with me?'

He shrugged. 'I'm not party to his plans, but he charged me with making you well again. That's a good sign for you, surely?'

Ren-*ya* sucked her teeth. If *Viktonovak* wanted her well, it was only so he could question her and find out where the totem was.

He picked up the lamp and held it close to her face. 'Those eyes of yours,' he said. 'Quite startling.' He stretched his hand out towards her and she flinched away. 'I won't hurt you. I'm a doctor.' He peered into her eyes. 'There was some bleeding back there, but it's stopped now.' He leaned down to examine Ren-*ya*'s bandaged leg. 'A nasty wound, but luckily the bullet missed the femur.' He brought his thumb and index finger together until they were almost touching. 'It was *that* close.'

He straightened up. 'Now get some rest. I'll let the

professor know you're back in the land of the living.'
He went over to the door and rapped on it. 'Coming
out!'

As the doctor stepped out, Ren-*ya* caught sight of
another man, a guard at her door.

Ren-*ya* slept through the day and didn't wake until late
in the evening when the door opened again and the
doctor came in with two guards.

'She can't walk,' he said. 'You'll have to carry her.'

After a lot of complaining about a bad back and
the number of stairs, the guards lifted Ren-*ya* out of
bed and put her on a chair that they then carried out
of the room.

The infirmary led on to a long corridor and from
there to the outside. Ren-*ya* barely had time to get a
sense of where she was, but she glimpsed a number of
wooden shelters arranged around the edge of a clearing.

In the middle of the clearing, a tall, square tower
rose up, taller than any of the forest trees that grew
around it. Ren-*ya* thought it must be the place where
Viktonovak lived. Her heart kicked in her chest as the
guards took her in through a doorway at the bottom.
Huffing and grunting with the effort, they carried
her up some wooden steps that curved inwards and
upwards, like the spiral shell of a sea creature.

At the top there was another door, this one guarded by men who carried the weapons Bela called 'guns'. They stepped aside and opened the door. Beyond was a dimly lit room with a fire basket smouldering in the middle. Behind it, lengths of sewn-together animal skins hung from roof to floor. There seemed to be nothing else in the room, but Ren-*ya*'s tongue tingled with a thick, peppery flavour. The taste of sickness. On top of that, as if someone was trying to mask it, the flavours of pine and juniper were heavy in the hot, still air.

The guards put the chair down, bowed towards the hangings and left.

A bright light flared behind the stretched pieces of hide that had been beaten so fine that Ren-*ya* could clearly see the silhouette of the person who held the light.

It must be him, *Viktonovak*, the man who had killed her mother.

Ren-*ya* cursed herself. Her enemy was no more than a few steps away, yet she had no weapon, no strength to do what had to be done.

The hangings parted a little, and a long-fingered hand covered in peeling skin emerged. 'I am Viktor Novak, the ruler of this world.' The fingers flexed and curled themselves into a fist, and it seemed to Ren-*ya* that it was the hand that spoke.

'Why are you keeping me here?' she said.

'Keeping you?' The fingers uncurled in a gesture of openness. 'You are a guest, not a prisoner.'

'Then why are there bars on the window and guards at the door?'

'We must protect ourselves. A guest might try to spy on her hosts.'

'I am no spy!' Ren-*ya* got a sudden urge to blurt it all out, to tell him she was there to avenge her mother, to kill him. But she bit down her anger and kept her thoughts to herself.

In the uneasy silence that followed, one thin, expressive finger rubbed itself against the flaking thumb. 'Very well. But I have some questions for you nonetheless . . . I wonder, what are you doing in this part of the forest?'

'I live here,' Ren-*ya* said. 'This place is *my* home. You and your followers are the intruders.'

The hand clenched and the knuckles whitened. 'And the girl? Isn't she an intruder in this world?'

Ren-*ya* could hear the sly smile in *Viktonovak*'s voice.

'So where is she hiding?' The hand opened expectantly, palm up, as if waiting to catch her answer. 'Is she close by?'

'I have nothing to say to you.'

The hand snapped shut like a trap, but the voice

became smooth, oily. 'Why make things more difficult than they need to be?'

Ren-*ya* knew what he was suggesting, the threat he was making. 'Do whatever you like,' she said. 'But I will never tell you anything.'

'So be it.' The hand slid back behind the hangings and he raised his voice. 'Call the guards.'

There was a movement in the gloom beside her and the hairs stood up on the back of Ren-*ya*'s neck. She realized there was someone standing in the corner of the room, a woman in a feather cloak. It was Eagle.

The spirit drew back her hood. She had the ochre eyes of a hawk and, instead of hair, her head was covered in tawny feathers. She turned towards the hangings and made a low bow. 'Whatever you command.' She stamped her foot twice and the guards came running. 'Take her to the cells.'

Ren-*ya* was carried from the room, down the snaking steps and out into the cold night. The guards took her to a long, low-roofed hut. Inside, the space was divided into cells and Ren-*ya* was roughly tipped on to the floor of one of these tiny pens.

'Sleep well,' one of the *white-eyes* said with a grin, shutting the barred door behind him.

It was dark, but Ren-*ya* could sense she was not alone. She could taste dog and *white-eye* on her tongue, the stink of rotten meat and sweat. But there was another flavour mixed in with the rest – the comforting scent of her own people's skin. Had the *white-eyes* captured one of the Last and brought them here?

She struggled into a sitting position. A shaft of pale moonlight shone through the bars in the door, illuminating a shadowy figure lying on the floor of the pen next to hers.

'Hey,' she whispered, but there was no reply.

Ren-*ya* dragged herself over to the dividing bars and, reaching through, gave the figure a shove.

There was a loud moan. 'Is it not enough to starve and beat me? Can I not even get some sleep?'

Ren-*ya* recognized the voice at once. 'Malor!'

THE GREAT WARRIOR

'Ren-*ya*?'

'Is it really you?' Ren-*ya* couldn't believe it. If there was anyone who could help her now, it was Malor, the man who had been her teacher. She pushed her hands through the bars and Malor took them in his. 'What are you doing here?' she said. 'We all thought you were dead.'

Malor spat on the floor. 'Not yet, although if the *white-eyes* have their way . . .'

The two of them swapped stories, and Ren-*ya* told Malor all about Bela and the totem.

'I have to get out of here,' Ren-*ya* said. 'She will not survive for long on her own.'

Malor sucked his teeth. 'Where is she now?'

Ren-*ya* glanced at him. There was no one in the world she trusted more, but she knew *Viktonovak* would stop at nothing to get the totem. 'In a safe place,' she said. 'But she is a *white-eye*, she has never had to hunt or fend for herself, and I have already been gone five days.'

'You left her with food?'

'Only a little.' She peered at him in the darkness. 'Tell me, how did those clumsy oafs manage to catch someone as clever as you?'

Malor cleared his throat. 'I was in my shelter, sleeping . . . And you?'

Ren-*ya* sighed. 'I sneaked up on them, but the breeze was in my face –'

'And you were attacked from behind?'

Ren-*ya* dipped her head. 'I know. After everything you taught me. It was stupid.'

Malor put his hand through the bars and took hers. 'We all make mistakes, Ren-*ya*. The important thing is Viktor Novak has not got the totem and you have not told him where to find it . . . yet.'

Ren-*ya* gritted her teeth. 'I will never tell.'

Malor gazed at her in the dawn light. After a moment, he nodded. 'We have to think of a way to get out of here.'

By morning, they had a plan, but they'd hardly added the finishing touches before two men came in and took Malor away. Ren-*ya* was afraid they'd be separated, but a few hours later they brought him back and threw him into his pen.

'What happened?' Ren-*ya* said when the men had gone.

Malor wiped the blood from a cut above his eye. 'The usual . . . and it will be your turn next.' He lowered his voice to a whisper. 'It has to be tonight.'

Once darkness had fallen and the camp was quiet, Ren-*ya* lay down, close to the bars that separated her pen from Malor's. She scraped dry earth from the floor and held it in her fist.

'Close your eyes,' Malor said. 'Leave everything to me.'

He got up and stood by the door to his cell. 'Guard!' he shouted. 'Come quickly, the girl is ill!'

There was a grating sound as the prison door swung open. 'I'm not falling for that one again.' Ren-*ya* recognized the voice – it was the captain. 'The girl's a faker – she can go ahead and die for all I care.'

'She is the only one who knows where the totem is,' Malor replied. 'If she dies, do you think Victor Novak will thank you?'

A moment later, the cell door creaked open and Ren-*ya* felt a firm nudge in her ribs – the toe of the captain's boot, she guessed. A bright light shone through her closed eyelids. She let out a loud moan and felt the captain's hands on her, rolling her over.

As she turned, Ren-*ya* threw the dust she was holding into his face. At the same time, Malor thrust his arms through the bars and clamped a hand over the captain's mouth, stifling his cry. He grabbed the knife from the captain's belt and plunged it into his neck. With a muffled groan, the soldier slumped to the floor.

Malor held up the knife. The blade flashed in the light, dripping with blood.

Ren-*ya* was horrified. She had seen many kills, and made many herself, only none had been so full of malice.

'Get the keys and put out the lamp,' Malor said.

Ren-*ya* prised the keys from the captain's clawed fingers. She limped to Malor's door and unlocked it.

Outside the prison, all was quiet. The moon was only a sliver in the sky, but around the edge of the clearing pine torches were mounted on wooden posts to light the dark night.

Malor pointed in the direction of the tower. 'The stables are round the back.'

Ren-*ya* looked up. She could see a light shining in a window at the top. That's where he was, up there, the man who killed her mother. She remembered how scornful she'd been when Bela told her how she'd stood over *Viktonovak*'s sleeping body with a knife. *Why didn't you kill him?* she'd said. Now she'd witnessed the slaughter of a human being, she knew how hard it was.

'Come on,' Malor said.

'I cannot leave without trying.'

'Trying what?'

'To kill him.'

'And how do you intend to do that?' Malor said. 'You are a child and you cannot even walk, but you are going to somehow get past his guards –'

Ren-*ya* spat into the snow. 'He killed my mother. He killed our people. Do they not deserve revenge?' She allowed a moment for this to sink in. 'Help me, Malor. You are a great warrior. You taught me to fight, to survive. I cannot do it, but you can.'

Malor sighed heavily. 'If only I had one or two good warriors with me . . .' He shrugged. 'But we are both injured. He has many guards with guns and we are bound to fail.'

'But –'

'Listen, Ren-*ya*. This *white-eye*'s time will come, and, I promise you, he will get all that he deserves. But that time is not now.'

Ren-*ya* stared at the ground. She knew he was right, but it hurt to give in.

'Come on.' Malor gave her a nudge. 'Think of your sister. We have to go.'

With Ren-*ya* leaning heavily on Malor's shoulder, they left the torchlight of the main compound behind them and made their way to a building behind a stand of trees.

Malor eased the door open. Inside, the room was lined with stalls and the air was thick with the warm, rich smell of animals, the huff of their breathing.

Malor led out two massive elk. He loaded the beasts up with straps and something he called a 'saddle'. Ren-*ya* was surprised he knew the words for the *white-eyes'* strange contraptions, but she reminded herself he had been a prisoner in the camp for many moons.

One of the elk reached its head out to Ren-*ya* and sniffed the top of her head. Suddenly it sneezed and Ren-*ya* jumped away. 'You want me to get on the back of this beast?'

Malor raised an eyebrow. 'You would rather walk on that leg?'

Ren-*ya* folded her arms. 'I suppose not.'

'Look, I shall keep hold of the reins,' Malor said. 'Put your foot in the stirrup here and then swing your other leg over its back.'

The elk's shoulder was at least a hand taller than Ren-*ya*, but with Malor's help she managed to scramble up and get her bad leg over the animal's broad back.

Malor climbed on to the back of the other elk in one smooth movement, as if he'd ridden before.

He gave a low whistle and the elk jerked into life and plodded out into the night.

Malor turned in the saddle and looked back at Ren-*ya*. 'So, which way?'

Ren-*ya* smiled. Now they were free, she could tell him. 'Towards the mountains,' she said. 'The Cave of the Spirits.'

Malor nodded. 'Of course. I should have thought of it before.' And then he lifted his head and howled like a wolf.

Ren-*ya* was bewildered. 'What are you doing?' she said. 'You will wake the camp!'

But before she could say any more, the dark shapes of men appeared from among the trees, surrounding them. They ran up and wrested the reins from Ren-*ya*'s hands.

'Malor!' she shouted, but he made no attempt to fight the *white-eyes* off, and when one of them came alongside his elk, they made a sign to each other that Ren-*ya* had never seen before – a straight hand touching one side of the forehead.

Her heart sank. Malor was one of them.

REMEMBRANCE

Bela was woken by the crackling of flames and the smell of root tea. She half opened her eyes and glimpsed a shadowy figure in the gloom. Suddenly she was wide awake, remembering the lion-headed man and his human transformation. She sat up.

He was there, over by the fire, dressed in sealskins. 'I thought you'd never wake up,' he said. 'You've been asleep for ages.'

Bela glanced down at her lap. The whalebone knife had gone.

He followed her gaze. 'I borrowed your knife to cut my beard and hair. I hope you don't mind.' He came towards her, but when Bela shrank back he stopped a few steps away. He held out the knife handle towards her. 'What happened before . . . I can't explain it. I'm sorry if I hurt you.'

Bela looked up at him. She told herself that, if he meant her harm, he could have killed her while she slept. She met his gaze and again had the feeling of having seen him somewhere before. His eyes were brown and she thought she saw kindness in them. But then she remembered Tron, how his evil presence came and went. He might still be hiding behind those soft-seeming eyes.

She put a hand to her neck and he flinched. 'Nothing like that will ever happen again. I promise . . .' He trailed off, gazing at her as she rubbed her neck. She realized he was staring at the totem and she tucked it down the front of her tunic, out of sight.

'Are you one of Viktor Novak's men?' she said.

'I'm not sure.' He frowned. 'Though the name sounds familiar.'

'Well, how did you get here then?'

He scratched his head. 'I don't know. It's starting to come back, in bits and pieces. That stone round your neck – seeing that made me remember I was human. It made me remember who I am.'

'And who would that be?'

'Sacha.' He snapped his fingers. 'The name came back to me as easy as that.'

Bela's heart thudded against her ribs. 'Sacha? Short for Alexander?'

'That's it! Alexander . . . ! Now, what was my other name . . . ?'

As he mumbled to himself, trying to remember, a sick feeling rose up in Bela's throat.

'I've got it!' He clapped his hands together. 'Novak! Alexander Novak! That's who I am.'

'No,' Bela said. 'You can't be.'

'Why not?'

'Alexander Novak is dead.'

He stared at her for a moment, perplexed. 'But I'm not dead, am I?'

Bela swallowed. 'No,' she whispered. 'You're not.' Her eyes searched his face. Could this man really be her father?

It was hard to think straight. He didn't know his beloved wife was dead. He didn't know his brother was the cause of all the misery in this world. He didn't even know that his daughter was right in front of his eyes.

'How do you know so much about me?' he said.

Bela turned her face away. More than anything, she wanted time to stand still. She wanted to leave, run away from the terrible truth that was unfolding itself in the darkness of the caves. She didn't want to be the one to tell him, but there was no one else to do it.

'You had a daughter,' she began.

'Yes! I remember. Her name is . . .' His fingers clutched at the air as if he was trying to pluck the memory from the darkness.

'Bela,' she whispered.

He looked up at her, frowning. 'What?'

'I'm *her*. I'm Bela.'

'No.' Sacha shook his head. 'You can't be – she's a baby.'

'I was a baby when you left, but now I've grown up. I'm thirteen.'

His gaze darted back and forth across her face.

Bela stumbled on. 'Not long after I was born, you went on an expedition and you never came back. Everyone said you were dead.'

'Bela . . .' He reached a hand out to touch her, but Bela shrank away and he drew his hand back as if it had been bitten.

For a while, they sat in silence, and then he said, 'But where's Nagar? Is she here?'

Bela covered her face with her hands. She couldn't look at him. It was unbearable to be the one to tell him what had happened to the woman he had loved.

'I'm sorry.' Tears flowed down Bela's cheeks and dripped into her lap. 'She died.'

His voice was small, as if it'd been strangled. 'How?'

'Viktor Novak. You said you remembered that name . . .' And then the rest came flooding out.

Sacha held his head in his hands as she told him what the professor had done to his wife, what he would have done to Bela if he'd had the chance.

'He's the one that caused all this,' she said. 'He's the reason I'm here. He's the reason *you're* here.'

Sacha raised his head. 'But he's my brother. Why would he do a thing like that?'

'He hates you,' Bela said. 'He's always hated you.'

Bela watched him out of the corner of her eye. She couldn't help searching his face for something of herself. And she found it, in the colour of his eyes, the shape of his ear, the curve of his dark eyebrows.

She turned it over and over in her head. Her father. What did that even mean? When he hadn't been there every day, caring for her as she grew up? Several times, he'd tried to talk about what she was like as a baby. She had to stop him, told him she didn't want to know. It was too painful for her to hear.

She didn't even know what she was supposed to call him. Daddy, Papa, Father? They were names she'd longed to use all her life, yet she couldn't imagine saying any of them to him now. *Sacha*, she decided. *I'll call him Sacha*.

He was bent over a pine branch, sharpening the end to a point with her knife. He worked with concentration, methodically. He'd been doing it for hours, ever since she told him. If he didn't stop whittling sticks, she was going to go mad.

He looked up suddenly and caught her studying him.

'So,' she said. 'Um . . . Sacha. I know this must all be a shock –'

He made a snorting noise, as if what she said couldn't have been more of an understatement.

'The thing is, we need to decide what to do.'

He grunted and went back to his whittling.

'Stop doing that!'

He looked hurt, but he put the stick down.

'I've been trying to tell you. Ren-*ya*'s been gone for days. We have to go and look for her.'

He picked up the stick and carefully shaved another sliver of wood from the point. 'Maybe it's best to wait here until she comes back.'

'Maybe she's in trouble and needs our help.' Bela said *our help*, but really she was thinking *my help*. She couldn't imagine him being much use. He didn't seem at all like the person who'd written the journal. He wasn't what she expected a father to be. 'Don't you want to make your brother pay for what he's done?'

He shrugged and removed another fine paring from the stick.

Bela watched him sink back inside his own world. He'd been alone in the darkness for so long and now he'd emerged to all this horror. She could taste the choking pain inside him. It was barely contained, like a wall of water behind a dam. The tiniest crack and it'd all come rushing out.

'It's too dangerous,' Sacha said. 'You should use the totem and go home.'

'And leave my sister and the Last at the mercy of your brother?'

'What can we do by ourselves? You said he has men, guns –'

'If it was the other way round, Ren-*ya* would never leave me. I can't let her down. Not Ren-*ya* and not my mother either.' She held his gaze. 'Don't forget, it was you who let your brother into this world in the first place.'

Sacha threw down his stick and started pacing back and forth in front of the fire. 'I can't let you put yourself in mortal danger. What kind of father would do that?'

Father. Bela flinched at the word. 'I've looked after myself for thirteen years,' she said. 'I'm not a baby any more.'

'No. I can't allow it.'

'Can't *allow* it?' Bela shook her head. 'Listen, you can come with me, or you can stay here, but first thing tomorrow I'm going out there to find my sister.' She got up and began to gather her things together.

Sacha slumped in front of the fire with his back to her, but after a while he came over to help. 'We'll need these,' he said, pointing to a pile of furs. 'It's cold out there.'

And at his words, a tiny chink opened in Bela's heart for him.

A LIFE'S WORK

The next day at dawn, Bela hunched down on a rock at the mouth of the cave and looked out across the trees. Ren-*ya* was somewhere out there. But where? The forest stretched as far as she could see in every direction.

She got up to go, but then turned back. She'd been inside the mountain for just a few days, but it felt as if a part of her had been left there forever. Sacha looked back too, and Bela wondered what he'd left behind in that heart of darkness.

'How did it happen?' she said to him. 'How did you become the lion-headed man?'

'It's all been coming back to me,' Sacha said. 'I was starving and sick, close to death. Somehow I found my way here. I survived by catching the blind white fish that live in the deep pools. These caves seemed a refuge at first, until I found the painting of the cave lion. I became obsessed and spent so long staring at it that the creature seemed to come alive. I felt a presence there, a spirit. It was distant at first, wary, but my fascination for the painting must have drawn it to me. I believe the spirit of the cave lion possessed me and made me forget who I was.'

Tentatively, Bela put her hand on his shoulder. 'Come on,' she said. 'It's time to go.'

They scrambled down the rocky cliff to the forest floor and Bela caught a flash of black and white ahead of her in the trees. It was the magpie, and for the first time in days she felt a surge of hope. The bird flew west, and Bela and Sasha followed.

At midday, they stopped to rest and shared the last scraps of food between them. As they ate, Sacha asked Bela how she had come to the spirit world and she told him about climbing over the roof and taking the totem back from the professor.

'You're so like your mother.' He smiled at her. 'She was just as resourceful and determined as you are.' Slowly, the smile slipped from his face. 'I can't believe she's really gone . . . I'm so sorry, Bela.'

'For what?'

'The more I remember, the more I realize that I'm the cause of all this. I wasn't the father, or the husband, that I should've been. I was far too concerned with myself, my career, my studies . . . She tried to warn me.'

'Nagar?'

He nodded. 'She never liked Victor. I couldn't understand it – he always seemed so kind and polite – but she begged me not to trust him. She used to say she could *taste* his deceit . . . If only I'd listened.' He hung his head. 'I already had everything: a loving wife, a beautiful child. But that wasn't enough for me, and I couldn't be satisfied until I'd come here and seen all this for myself.'

'Didn't she try to stop you?'

'Oh yes. She didn't want me to go. She said the totem wasn't created to satisfy *my* curiosity.' A look of anguish crossed his face. 'But I was so arrogant, so sure I was right. I wore her down, ranting on and on about science, the nobility of knowledge and learning. I'm ashamed to say it, but I told her, since she couldn't read and write, that she would never understand my higher calling.' He hid his face in his hands. 'What a fool I've been. My vanity has caused all this. And all my books and learning, what use are they to anyone now?'

*

They set off again, but by the afternoon they were cold and exhausted and they stopped on the shore of a frozen lake for the night. They'd eaten nothing all day but berries and pine nuts, and Sacha said he'd try to catch a fish.

He went out on to the ice, cutting a hole at the edge where it was thinnest. When Bela had finished building the shelter, he called her over.

'Look,' he said, showing her the harpoon he intended to use. 'Look at the workmanship.'

Bela held it in her hand. Like the handle of her knife, it was made of bone. A series of triangular points, like fins, had been carved along its length on either side, each one decorated with a pattern of dots and stripes. 'Where did you find it?'

'In the caves,' he said. 'The detail's amazing, isn't it? It would've been carved with nothing more than a stone tool.'

Bela looked up into his rapt face. For the first time, she glimpsed the man who'd written the journals, the father she wished she'd known.

She handed the harpoon back. 'What you said earlier – you're being too hard on yourself. It wasn't vanity that made you come here.'

Sacha looked up at her. 'Why do you say that?'

She smiled. 'I read your journals.'

'Did you?'

Bela reached out and took his hand. 'The things you wrote, they meant a lot to me. It was your journals that made me want to come here. Your work meant a lot to Eva too. You inspired her and she stayed on at Wilder House to catalogue your artefacts.'

'I suppose it's good to know it wasn't all for nothing, that someone as able as Eva is carrying on with it.'

'You can carry on with it yourself, when we get home.'

'Home?' For a moment, he stared off into the distance, but then he shook his head. 'I have no home.'

'Yes, you do. Eva and Arno are there. Everything's still there – your books, your artefacts, all your life's work.'

'Let's not talk of home any more.' Sacha turned away and gazed off into the forest. The choking flavour of dust hung in the air, as if the battle between Nort and Tron still raged inside him. But after a while the taste of his torment ebbed away. He smiled and squeezed her hand. 'You're the only thing that matters to me now. You're my life's work.'

They stayed out on the lake together, taking turns with the harpoon. The light began to fail, but hunger

drove them on and, just before it got dark, Sacha managed to spear a fat salmon. The pair of them threw their arms round each other and danced about on the ice.

That night, Bela fell asleep happy, with a full belly.

THE REAL HERO

Viktonovak's men dragged Ren-*ya* from her mount and forced her to her knees in front of Malor.

'How could you do this?' she said.

Malor hardly glanced at her. He turned to his men. 'Take her back to the camp.'

Ren-*ya*'s hands were tied and the rope attached to the saddle of one of the soldiers. She was jerked along behind his mount and forced to stumble back to the camp as best she could.

Once there, she was thrown on the ground at the foot of *Viktonovak*'s tower. The light was still burning in the window at the top and, for a moment, a shadowy face wavered there, looking down at her.

His hand appeared in the window and he made

some sign to the soldiers below. They each took one of Ren-*ya*'s arms, dragged her to the prison and locked her in the cell again.

Ren-*ya* struggled to her feet. 'I want to see Malor.'

One of the men smirked. 'I dare say, but I doubt the colonel wants to see you.'

'*Colonel*?'

'Aye,' the man said. 'He's second in command, after the professor.'

When the men had gone, Ren-*ya* slumped to the floor. The bitter taste of treachery made her want to be sick. How could she have been so stupid? Her blind belief in Malor – it was just like sneaking up on prey with the breeze in her face.

She looked round the filthy cell. There was no way to get out. Her gaze came to rest on the place where the captain had fallen. His body was gone, but there was a dark stain on the earth floor and the stink of death lingered in the air.

That night, she hardly slept. The acrid taste of Malor's betrayal kept her awake, burning her tongue.

At dawn *Viktonovak*'s men came. They tied her hands, dragged her out of the prison and threw her in a cart shackled to an elk. A group of mounted *white-eyes* were lined up in front, led by Malor. He was dressed in the same clothes as the *white-eyes* and Ren-*ya* saw how they deferred to him, called him *colonel*.

'Bring the carriage,' Malor commanded.

A black vehicle rolled into the clearing, pulled by two elks. It stopped at the bottom of the tower and Ren-*ya* caught a glimpse of the man wrapped in furs climbing in. Ren-*ya* narrowed her eyes. *Viktonovak* . . . and climbing into the carriage with him was Eagle.

Ren-*ya* hung her head. They had all betrayed her. First Eagle, the guardian spirit of the Last, and now Malor, the man who taught her to survive the *long winter*, the greatest warrior her people had ever known.

Travelling by elk was almost as slow as going on foot and the *white-eyes* spent two days manoeuvring *Viktonovak*'s carriage through thick forest and across frozen rivers. Sometimes, when they came to a particularly difficult patch of ground, the *white-eyes* would have to dismount, unshackle the elks from the carriage and carry it themselves.

The journey was a misery for Ren-*ya*. With every jolt of the cart, and there were many, her leg fizzed with pain. But the wound was nothing to the anguish she felt. She had led them to Bela. It didn't matter that she hadn't meant to. It seemed to Ren-*ya* that whatever she did, however hard she tried, she was defeated by lies.

Despite the slow pace, the distant snow-topped mountains grew ever larger, ever nearer, and on the second evening they reached the foothills and set up camp.

Early the next morning, they carried Ren-*ya* to the foot of the mountain and up to the caves. She felt tired and fragile, not just from her injuries, but from the sickness in her heart. When they got to the mouth of the caves, Malor and two of the *white-eyes* went off ahead into the tunnels. Ren-*ya* was left waiting at the entrance with the rest of *Viktonovak*'s men for the longest hour of her life.

But when Malor and the others returned, Bela was not with them. Malor grabbed Ren-*ya* by the arm and dragged her to her feet. He stuck his face in hers. 'Where is she? Where is the girl?'

'I do not know.' Relief swept through Ren-*ya* like a storm. Somehow her sister and the totem were gone.

Ren-*ya*'s hands and feet were bound. She was dragged inside the mountain, thrown into a tiny cave and left there in the dark. But Ren-*ya* couldn't help smiling as she imagined Malor having to tell *Viktonovak* that Bela could not be found.

Several hours went by and then Malor appeared with a lamp. 'I will ask you just once more – where is she?'

Ren-*ya* blinked in the sudden brightness. 'I already told you. I do not know.'

Malor came into the cave and squatted down next to her. He put the lamp down on the floor and dark shadows pooled beneath his eyes. 'You might find this hard to believe, but I was trying to help you back there. Viktor Novak would have had you killed straight off, only I said you were more useful alive.'

'What do you want?' Ren-*ya* said. 'Thanks?'

'He might still let you live if you tell us where she is.'

Ren-*ya* laughed and shook her head.

'Do not play the hero,' Malor said. 'It never suited you.'

'It suits you even less.'

In the dim light, they stared at each other. Malor was the one to look away.

'Why, Malor?' Ren-*ya* said. 'What made you do it?'

His eyes widened. 'I want to live again. Not here, in this shadow-of-a-life.' He looked at her. 'Maybe you can understand, you who will never grow up. You are stuck, the same as me.'

Ren-*ya* spat on the floor.
His self-pity made her sick.
'There are a lot of things
I would do to grow up, but
betraying my people is not one
of them.'

Malor shook his head. 'Listen,
everything I have done is for us, for the
Last. I have done it to fulfil the prophecy.
Tell me where the girl is and we will get the
totem. Viktor Novak has promised to take me
back to the waking world . . . I will persuade
him to take you too if you help.' He stared off into
the darkness. 'He has told me all about that other
world. It is nothing like ours. Their world is full of
light, even in the darkest night. I long to see it. I yearn
to see the future.'

Ren-*ya* laughed bitterly. 'For a man who cannot
keep his own promises, you have a lot of faith in the
promises of others.' She leaned towards him and took
his hand. 'Listen to me, Malor. He is lying to you. He
has made you a "colonel", made you feel important –
but think, Malor! Think what he will do to the girl if he
finds her. Do you want her death on your conscience?
Her death *and* mine?'

Malor wrenched his hand away, but Ren-*ya*

persisted. 'I used to think the world of you. We all did. You could be a real hero, the sort who is never forgotten, the sort we would sing about on cold winter nights –'

'You think I care about being a hero, about being "good"? What has goodness done for you? It only made you easier to fool.'

He stood and picked up the lamp. 'I will ask you one more time. Where is she?'

'I do not know, and even if I did, I would never tell you.'

He sighed. 'Well, I have done my best to help you. Victor Novak will get the truth one way or another.' He turned to go.

'Just one more thing,' Ren-*ya* said. 'That man, the guard. Did you really kill him or was that another trick?'

Malor turned to face her. 'It was no trick.'

'But he was on your side.'

His black eyes met Ren-*ya*'s, but they couldn't rest there and he looked away again. 'He was not important. Sacrifices have to be made.'

CROW

In the middle of the night, Bela was woken by a chattering sound. Carefully, so as not to wake Sacha, she slid out from underneath the furs, pulled on her boots and went outside. There was a rush in the air and the magpie landed on her shoulder. It rubbed its head on her cheek and then flew off into the trees.

There was only a paring of moon and the night was dark. Bela fetched the lamp, lit it from the embers of the fire and set off in the direction in which the bird had flown. She was led into the depths of the forest, where the trees grew close together. The branches closed over her head, shutting out the sky and the bright stars. She held the lamp up and the light sent black shadows flowing between the trunks of the pines, gliding over the snow. The trees loomed out of the night, then parted before her. Their long shadows crept round her like predators before slinking away into the darkness.

A few times she faltered, once when a strange scream, like the drawn-out cry of a child, lifted the hairs on the back of her neck. 'Only a fox,' she whispered to herself.

The moon had risen high into the sky by the time Bela emerged from thick forest. Ahead of her was a clearing with a single tall tree standing in the middle. The bird was perched in the topmost branches.

There was a sound like someone clearing their throat, and then a voice. 'Climb up.'

Bela stepped back in alarm. 'Who . . . who's there?'

'Climb up and you will see.'

'Why? What are you doing up a tree?' Bela asked.

'I live here.'

'Oh well, can't you . . . come down here?' she said.

'No.' There was a gravelly chuckle. 'Climb up and you will see why not.'

Bela peered up through the branches. She thought she saw the pale flash of a face, but she couldn't be sure. She put the lamp down on the ground.

'Bring the light,' came the voice. 'I want to be able to see you properly.'

Bela hooked the handle of the lamp over her arm and began to climb. There were plenty of sturdy branches at regular intervals, but the problem was how to force a way up through the mass of smaller twigs and pine needles. *Who would want to live in a tree?* she thought as she climbed, her hair and clothes snagging on every branch.

Close to the top, she looked up. She could just make out a shadowy, wizened face looking down at her.

'Come closer,' the creature said.

She climbed until she drew level.

'Lift the lamp,' it said. 'Let me see you.'

Bela held it between them in her shaking hand. It shone on the creature's face, sparkling on the ice crystals that clung to its skin. Its features were perfectly preserved, even the matted lashes that fringed its swollen eyelids. But the creature was not whole. Its shrunken neck finished in tattered blackened flesh where a body should've been. There was only a head hanging in the branches by its tangled hair.

Its bruised lips cracked open. 'There is no need to be afraid. I wish you no harm and, as you see, I have no limbs with which to hurt you.'

Bela swallowed down her fear. 'Shouldn't you be . . . dead?'

The creature cackled. 'A spirit cannot be killed, and anyway this is the land of the dead – where would we go?'

'You're a spirit?'

'I am Crow.'

Bela remembered Hebera mentioning the spirit's name. 'The Last say you abandoned them.'

'I did no such thing! Eagle, Raven and I *found* this world. My sisters and I are the guardians of the Last.'

Bela gritted her teeth. 'Eagle is our enemy. She's betrayed her people.'

The creature's eyes rolled up in its head. 'She did not betray them. She is Viktor Novak's slave and cannot help what she is made to do.' It licked its lips with a pointed tongue. 'That is the story I have called you up this tree to hear. Come closer and I will tell you.'

With the blood beating in her ears, Bela edged a little nearer.

'Good,' the creature said. 'Now listen. When Viktor Novak invaded our world, he captured me. He promised to let me go if my sister would tell him her true name in return.'

'Eagle?'

'That is one of her names, but each spirit has a name that speaks to our heart, a name that gives complete power to the person who knows it.'

'And she told him?'

'She did.' The creature smiled. 'I expect you, more than anyone, to understand that a person will do anything to save a sister.'

Bela nodded. 'What happened?'

'Eagle kept her side of the bargain, but Viktor Novak is not an honourable man. He does not keep his promises. Straight away, he told his men to cut my head from my body and throw both pieces into the lake.' A slow smile crept on to the spirit's face. 'But if you want something done right, you should do it yourself. It was a cold night and the ice was thick. They could not be bothered to cut a hole, so they dragged me here instead, left my body for the beasts and tossed my head into this tree, where I have been stuck ever since . . . Even so, it was a big mistake.'

'Why?'

'Because now here I am, talking to you.' The creature winked one rheumy eye. 'And I could not do that if my head was at the bottom of a lake.'

'No,' Bela said uncertainly. 'I suppose not.'

'Listen, I may not have the powers my sister has, but I am not without talents. If I close my eyes, I see what is happening far away. Not just in space, but in time too.'

'And what do you see?'

The creature closed one eye. 'I see Viktor Novak. I see where he is right now.'

'Where?'

'In the caves. He got there just a few hours after you left.' The creature grinned, showing the blackened stumps of her teeth. 'I have seen your sister too.'

Bela almost toppled out of the tree. 'Where? Where is she?'

'Sad to say, she is Viktor Novak's prisoner. But at least she has learned a valuable lesson about trust . . . and betrayal.'

Bela clenched her fists. 'I would never betray her.'

'Nor she you, *suran-ya*.'

The name reminded Bela of the promises she and Ren-*ya* had made. 'How can I help her? Tell me what to do.'

'Only you can decide, but I will tell you this much – Viktor Novak has sent Eagle out into the forest to look for you. There is only one way to escape. You carry the totem and I can open the doorway between the worlds for both you and your father. But if you do not leave this world tonight, Eagle will find you before the dawn.' The creature opened her black eyes wide. 'You came here to find out who you are. Before this day is out, you will have your answer. Now go.' The spirit's swollen eyes slid shut. 'Do what you must.'

RETURN TO THE
HEART OF DARKNESS

Bela followed the magpie back to the frozen lake. The first light of dawn was bleeding out of the horizon and the edge of the world had turned from black to darkest blue. Dawn was coming fast and she must decide what to do. She remembered Hebera's foretelling, that she and Ren-*ya* would make a promise and face a test, that each of them must save the other. *You came here to find out who you are*, that's what Crow had said.

Bela knew she could return to the waking world that very night. She'd be safe, but it would mean leaving Ren-*ya*, and although she was afraid of what was to come, she knew she could not choose to do that. *Do what you must*, Crow had said. There wasn't much time left, but Bela already knew what she had to do.

She lifted the flap of hide that covered the door of the shelter and peered in. Sacha was inside, fast asleep. She would've liked to wake him, tell him where she was going, but she knew he'd try to stop her. She took the totem from her neck and laid it on the ground next to him, where it glittered darkly, as if warning her of what was to come. Soon Eagle would find her and take her to Viktor Novak. After that, Bela didn't know what would happen, but she was sure of one thing – her uncle mustn't be allowed to get his hands on the totem again.

She turned to go, but at the last minute she took the whalebone knife out of her pocket and left it in the shelter alongside the totem. She had a feeling Sacha would need it more than her.

Before she left, Bela wrote a single word in the snow outside the door of the shelter – CAVES. Then she shouldered her pack and began the journey to the mountains, towards Eagle and the coming dawn.

The magpie flew alongside her as if he knew his presence gave her courage, and when she held her hand out, the bird flew to her.

'What do you think?' Bela said, stroking his glossy feathers. 'Am I doing the right thing?'

The bird ducked its head. It seemed to be an answer, but was it a yes or a no? Suddenly the magpie gave a warning call and flew away.

A black-headed eagle descended from the sky and landed in the top of a tree. It turned its piercing eyes on Bela and, spreading its great wings, leaped from the branches. As it plunged to the ground, it began changing from bird to human and, by the time it came to land, its wings had become a dark, feathered cloak and its talons human feet. But its eyes were not human. They were golden, the eyes of a raptor.

The spirit held out her hand. 'Come, *suran-ya*.'

Bela's body lurched forward of its own accord and it took all her will to stop herself taking another step. 'Wait! Crow says you didn't abandon the Last. She told me you're a slave.'

Eagle bowed her feathered head. 'Crow speaks the truth.'

'Can't you fight against him, the power he has over you?'

Eagle looked into Bela's face. 'Your mother was truly loved and it gives me no pleasure to hunt her daughter down like prey. I live for the time when I will be free again.' She clenched her clawed hand into a fist. 'Then I will crush him. I will grind his bones to dust.' Bela caught the taste of Eagle's fury: the stink of burning hair. 'Come, *suran-ya*, for I am yet a slave and must take you to him.'

Eagle opened her cloak, and Bela again felt the creature draw her in. This time, Bela did not resist. She had made her choice and she willingly walked towards Eagle's outstretched arms, let herself be wrapped in the spirit's fearful embrace.

*

Eagle did not release Bela from her grip until they were back inside the mountain, deep in the caves. There, Eagle handed her over to the professor's men.

One of them forced Bela down a twisting tunnel that opened into a shallow-roofed cavern. The light inside was dim, coming from a single lamp and a smouldering brazier that threw moving shadows on to the enclosing walls.

On the other side of the fire, a figure sat alone in the gloom. He was wrapped in furs, hunched up like an invalid. He lifted his head and turned towards her. His face had changed. His eyes were sunken and his skin was cracked as if he'd aged many years. But the cold blue eyes were just the same. They stared out at her from his ruined face, sizing her up, working out what she was worth, as cruel and hungry as ever. 'Wait outside,' he said to the soldier. 'No one is to be admitted under any circumstances.'

The soldier gave a small bow and left.

'Look at me,' the professor said, and Bela forced herself to meet his gaze.

He stood with difficulty. 'Do you see how sick I am? Do you see what has become of me without the totem, without the blood I need?'

Bela remained silent.

'Well?' he shouted.

'You brought all this on yourself,' Bela replied.

'What an ungrateful wretch you are! I made you my ward, took you into my home, and this is how you repay me?'

'Don't pretend it was a kindness. I know very well why you summoned me to Wilder House. My fate would've been the same as my mother's.'

The professor shook his head. 'I did her a favour. I kept her away from the gaze of the outside world, didn't I? Imagine if anyone had got even a glimpse of those freakish eyes.'

'I don't see how it could have gone any worse for her than it did.'

The professor made a sweeping gesture, as if he'd lost patience with the argument. 'Why should you care? You never even knew her.'

'Only because you and Aunt Olga tore us apart.'

'It was for your own good. Nagar was hardly human, a freak of nature. We hoped you might turn out differently.' He sighed. 'Sadly, you have inherited your mother's savagery.' He gazed at her for a moment. 'You look human, but deep down, under your skin, you're a thing that was never meant to be.'

Once, those words might have hurt Bela. There was even a time when she had thought herself a freak. But not any more. She was descended from a clan who survived on their courage and their wits, and she would never be ashamed of it again.

'Your mother was no more than an animal,' the professor continued. 'We are the superior species! Her kind died out thousands of years ago.'

He took a few limping steps towards her, then paused next to the brazier. He stretched his fingers out to warm them and, as he rubbed his hands together, his cloak trailed close to the embers. Bela imagined a lick of flame touching the furred edge of the cloak. It would smoulder at first, then catch hold. In her mind's eye, she saw the flames race up, torching his dried-out skin, engulfing his body. He would burn up until nothing was left of him. Only blackened, papery flakes floating on the air, a smoky stain on the cavern floor.

The professor's voice brought her back to reality. 'You've led me a merry dance, my dear, but now the thief is caught.'

'I'm no thief.'

'You stole the totem from me while I slept.'

'It belongs to the Last.'

'No!' He slammed his fist into his palm. 'It is mine!'

'You're a rich man in your own world – don't you already have enough?'

'Wealth means nothing. Here I have *power*. Here I am king, and all must obey me or die. With the totem and your blood, I can live here forever.' A small smile twitched at the corner of his mouth. 'It also gives me great pleasure to spoil the things my brother loved so dearly.'

'Things' like my mother, Bela thought.

'So,' the professor said. 'Where is the totem?'

Bela gritted her teeth. 'It isn't yours.'

He looked back at her coolly. 'There's an easy way to do this and there's a hard way . . . I have a prisoner here. Someone I think you know?'

Bela's voice broke in the echoing cave. 'What have you done to her?'

The professor shrugged. 'I had no choice; she wouldn't tell me where you were.'

'She didn't know!'

'Maybe you're right, but it's hard to tell with someone as stubborn as her. I'd say you got here just in time, or there wouldn't have been much left of her . . . Now, do you want to save her life or don't you?'

Bela closed her eyes. 'I don't know where it is.'

'Well, one of you must know. Either you or that savage girl, although –' he made as if to leave – 'I'm not sure she can take much more questioning.'

Bela grabbed his arm. 'Please don't hurt her.'

He shrugged her off. 'It's up to you. Either you get the totem for me now, or she dies.'

'It's not mine to give.'

The professor leaned in until his face was only inches from hers. 'You have no choice,' he said. 'The Last, your so-called "people", are doomed. I am building an eternal empire. I have guns and men, and what do you have? Nothing. Nothing and no one –'

Suddenly a voice came out of the gloom. 'I wouldn't say that, brother.'

The professor spun round. 'Who's there?'

Sacha stepped out of the shadows and Bela's heart leaped. 'It's me, brother. Surely you haven't forgotten?'

The professor's mouth hung open before he regained his senses. 'Guard!' he shouted. 'Guard!'

'Shout as loud as you like.' Sacha held up the whalebone knife, its blade streaked with blood. 'No one's coming.'

The professor slipped his arm round Bela's neck and forced her between him and Sacha. 'Stay where you are!' He took a knife from his pocket and pressed the tip of the blade against her throat. 'One step closer and

I'll kill the girl.' He drove a hand into Bela's hair and twisted it round his wrist, holding her fast. She felt the chill of the blade against her skin and held her breath, afraid to make the slightest move.

'I thought you were dead,' Viktor said.

Sacha gave him a small, cold smile. 'You mean, you thought you'd killed me.'

'How did you get in here?'

'There are many ways in if you know where to look.' Sacha's voice was low and even, but Bela could taste the rage buried in it. 'This mountain was my home. I rotted here for years because of you.'

The professor shook his head. 'Why blame me? You want the same things I do, only you wanted them all to yourself.'

'Yes, to study, to understand. But not to conquer, not to kill.'

Sacha took a step forward and the professor tightened his grip on Bela. 'Stay where you are or I'll kill her.'

Sacha held up his hands. 'No need for that, brother. I'm sure we can come to an arrangement. Just tell me what it is you want.'

'The totem.'

'It's right here,' Sacha said. 'Inside this very mountain.'

Bela licked her lips. The oily flavour on her tongue confirmed what she'd already guessed: Sacha was bluffing, laying a clever trap.

But the professor's desperation made him blind to the deception and his breathing quickened. 'You'll take me to it?'

'If you let my daughter go.'

'I'll let her go, and that savage sister of hers too . . . but only when the totem is safely in my hands.' He paused for a moment. 'If you're lying . . .' He twisted Bela's head. 'One cut, that's all it would take. Now throw your knife down over there.'

Sacha dropped it to the floor.

'Take this light.' The professor pushed the lamp towards him with his foot. 'Lead the way.'

Sacha leaned down and picked it up. 'Whatever you say, brother.'

The professor pushed Bela towards the entrance of the cave, keeping her body between him and Sacha. They made their way like this into the maze of branching tunnels. After a while, they entered a passageway where the salt crystals glimmered in the lamplight like diamonds, and Bela knew she'd been there before. Sacha led them on, to where the tunnel split in two, choosing the left fork and, at the end of that, the right.

Around the corner the drawings of the cave lion and the painted hands were waiting for them in the twisting labyrinth. The taste of the lion-man's torment, the choking flavour of dust, burned on Bela's tongue.

Sacha hesitated as they passed by. He lifted the lamp to gaze at the frenzied images and for a moment a look of horror crossed his face. Then he drew his lips together in a narrow line, as if some hard and terrible decision had been made. He plunged on, deeper into the mountain, and soon the paintings were lost behind them in the darkness.

Bela wished that she'd asked him about them, why he had made them, what they meant to him. She promised herself that, when this was over, she'd let him know she understood the pain that had created them. She would tell him there was no need to torment himself. She would let him know that she forgave him.

This is where it ends

After that, Sacha didn't stop. At the end of each corridor, as the tunnel split, he chose the way with certainty. He moved quickly and the professor, in his weakened state, with one hand buried in Bela's hair, struggled to keep up. 'How much further?' he said.

Sacha turned back with a faint smile on his lips. 'It's a labyrinth, brother. These tunnels go on forever – if you got lost in here, you'd never find your way out again, but I expect you've been counting the turnings?'

Her uncle's hand tightened round Bela's hair, and she knew he hadn't. It wasn't a mistake she would ever make again, but this time she knew where Sacha was taking them.

They continued in silence until Sacha came to a sudden halt.

The professor dragged Bela back against the cave wall. 'What is it? Why have you stopped?'

Sacha turned back to them and held up the lamp. The flame wavered and smoked. 'See that? We're running out of oil. But there's no need to worry. I know my way there in the dark.'

Bela heard the catch in the professor's breath. The rancid taste of his fear reminded her of the vision she'd seen in the *smoke*. The small boy screaming in the darkness, begging to be let out. 'He's afraid,' she managed to choke out. 'He's afraid of the dark.'

'Shut up!' The professor pressed the tip of his blade against Bela's throat.

Sacha narrowed his eyes. There was something about the flickering light and the shadows it threw on her father's face, something in the tone of his voice that reminded Bela of the monster he'd been. 'Ah yes. I'd forgotten, brother, how frightened you are of the dark.'

The professor just stood there, breathing hard, and Sacha laughed softly. 'Surely you remember? When you were a boy, you would wake up in the night, crying. You wouldn't stop until Mother brought a lamp. She used to laugh at you, call you a baby. I always wondered

333

myself how you seemed so brave during the day, yet such a coward at night.'

The professor's breath wheezed in his throat.

'You wouldn't like it here,' Sacha continued. 'Here the night goes on forever, one eternal stretch of darkness without the sanity that daylight brings.' He held the lamp up between them. 'Look at this tiny flame. It's the only thing that's keeping the darkness and all that madness at bay. But it's running out; it's dying.' He peered at his brother in the dim light. 'It must be terrifying for someone like you, a man who can't bear to be contained.' He stretched his hand up and touched the roof of the tunnel. 'All that rock, all that weight above our heads. It's almost as if it compresses the air, makes it thicker, makes it harder to breathe.'

The professor gasped and coughed. The breath rattled in his chest.

Sacha opened the glass door of the hurricane lamp. 'I could blow it out right now and the dark will come for us, swallow us up.'

The professor forced Bela's head back against his shoulder. The blade trembled against her skin. 'If you do that,' he whispered, 'I'll kill her.'

Sacha snapped the door shut on the quivering flame. 'No need for that, brother. Didn't I say? We're almost there.'

*

Bela heard the sucking sounds of the whirlpool long before they got to the low-roofed cavern.

Sacha ducked through the entrance and walked to the brink of the pool. As he lifted the lamp, their three dark shadows crept over the rocks and climbed the walls. He stared down into the black water. 'There's not much time left, brother.'

'Is this the place? Is this where you've hidden it?'

'No, brother. This is where it ends. There's no way out of this place for you, and none for me either.'

'Have you forgotten our bargain?' he said. 'Have you forgotten about *her*?'

'No, I haven't forgotten.' Sacha's eyes met Bela's and he held her gaze. 'She's my daughter, the child I held in my arms. She is the only thing left, the only thing that matters to me in the whole world.' He turned away. 'But you can only take one of us down with you. Who would you rather be left with when the flame has gone out and you're lost in the dark?'

When Sacha turned back, Bela saw his face had changed. There was no kindness left and no fear. Everything had been wiped away.

He put the lamp down on the ground at his feet and his face disappeared into the darkness. Now all Bela could see of him were his eyes – two fiery amber points of light – the eyes of the cave lion.

'Do you remember?' Sacha said.

Bela's throat seemed to close up. She'd heard that voice before, saying those very same words. Tron was still here in the dark, still alive in the labyrinth of her father's broken mind.

'Do you remember our mother?' Sacha said. 'You loved her, didn't you? There was a happy time, a wonderful time, when it was just you and her . . . until I was born. Do you remember looking at me for the first time? A tiny bundle of joy, wrapped up in blankets, asleep in her arms. *Isn't he beautiful?* Was that what she said?' His eyes flared, gold in the darkness. 'But a monstrous jealousy gripped your heart. It was so strong, so terrible, that you couldn't even explain it to yourself. The truth was she loved someone else more than you.'

A strange sound escaped from the professor's throat, a child's fearful sob.

Sacha took a step forward and his shadow grew, dwarfing the professor's on the wall of the cave. 'I can only imagine how painful it must've been,' he said, 'as gradually, bit by bit, I edged you out, replaced you in her affections. You tried to prove yourself to her, to show that you were better, more deserving than me, cleverer. But she saw you for what you are. A dark and twisted heart, nothing more than an empty shell. She ⌐erated you, but she couldn't love you, and all your desperation only pushed her further and further away.'

He paused, as if waiting to see the effect of what he'd said. 'What do you think of my analysis, Professor? There's an abandoned child under the skin of every evil man, and there can't be a single person alive who knows that better than you. Isn't it true? Aren't *I* the one who's made you what you are?'

The professor's grip on Bela loosened. He seemed to strain towards Sacha and the dying light.

'It's time, brother. The darkness is coming.' Sacha reached inside his parka, took the totem from his neck and held it out in front of him. The crystal had never looked more alluring. It shone in the gloom, swirled with eddies of golden light. 'If you want it, come and get it.'

The professor's fingers slipped from Bela's hair and

the cave echoed with his tormented cry as he launched himself towards the edge of the water.

Sacha dropped the totem to the floor and opened his arms to receive him. They could have been two brothers embracing if it hadn't been for the cries of anger, the flash of gritted teeth. The professor twisted and fought, trying to reach the totem on the ground, while with every second that passed Sacha dragged him closer and closer to the whirlpool's edge.

For a moment, they seemed to be held there, swaying together on the brink, neither able to gain the advantage . . . only the professor still had his knife, and Bela saw with horror that he was working the hand that held it from Sacha's grip. Any minute now, he would free his weapon.

At that moment, Bela realized that, in showing her the professor's fear of the dark, the *smoke* had gifted her the way to defeat him. She ran forward and grabbed the lamp.

It made her remember the lamp she'd held before, in this very cave, when she chose between the darkness and her own life. Only this time, the flickering flame was *the professor's* life. It leaped and flared like the beating of his evil heart.

Bela blew the flame out.

There was a cry of terror, of rage, cut dead by the roar of swirling water, and the darkness rushed in and closed its fist around them.

THE WISDOM OF THE SPIRITS

Bela crawled on her hands and knees, feeling around on the cold rock floor until her fingers fumbled on the totem. She picked it up, felt its heavy warmth in her hand, and in her mind's eye she held the sorrow on her father's face as he let it drop.

It was the last she saw of him. She was glad that in the darkness she did not have to watch him fall. She did not have to see him sucked down beneath the black water. He'd given his life for her. He was a good man, a good father – she knew that now.

She raised her head at an approaching light and saw Eagle standing in the tunnel beyond the cavern, holding a burning torch.

'There is no need to be afraid,' the spirit said. 'I am

not Viktor Novak's creature any longer.'

Bela got to her feet. 'What are you doing here?'

'I came to find you. And to return this.' She handed her the whalebone knife.

'Where's my sister?' Bela said.

'She is safe and well.'

'And my uncle's men?'

'Two are dead by my hand and the rest have run away, Malor among them.'

'Malor? I thought he was dead.'

Eagle shook her head. 'Come, *suran-ya*. I will take you to Ren-*ya* and explain all that has happened along the way.'

Bela followed Eagle through the twisting tunnels of the labyrinth. When they reached the drawing of the cave lion and the wall of painted hands, Eagle stopped and kneeled down.

'What are you doing?'

'I give thanks to the lion-headed man.' She lifted the torch high above her tawny-feathered head and the painted hands seemed to come to life, seemed to stream across the cave wall.

But to Bela, they were no longer searching for escape. In the trembling light, they flitted across the rock like a flock of flying birds, wild and free.

'This place was a shrine to his humanity,' Eagle said. 'He returned here time and time again to mourn what he had lost.' She bowed her head. 'His pain is buried here at last. He is free now . . . and he has set me free too.'

Bela placed her own palm on top of one of the painted hands. Hers was smaller and fitted easily inside. She could still taste the ochre pigment, but the choking flavour of the lion-man's torment had disappeared and she knew her father's spirit was gone from this world.

Eagle led Bela through the winding tunnels to a cavern where pitch torches burned their smoky breath into the rock. 'In there,' she said. 'I will leave the two of you alone.'

Ren-*ya* was inside, lying on a pile of furs. Her face was covered in bruises and one leg was bandaged and propped up. Despite her injuries, she struggled to her feet to make the proper greeting, and pressed her palm against Bela's. 'Our mother is avenged and her spirit is at peace at last.' She drew back a little. 'I am sorry your father lost his life for this.'

'Thank you,' Bela replied. 'I believe he too has found peace.'

For a moment, the sisters stood in silence. Then, the formalities over, they threw their arms round each other and began to exchange stories, recounting all that had happened since they were last together in the caves.

Ren-*ya* said, 'It must have been a shock to find your father was alive all along.'

Bela nodded. 'The long dark years alone had changed him, but in his heart he was still the same good man.'

Ren-*ya* gazed at her. 'You could have gone back to your own world,' she said. 'Your father would still be alive now if you had.'

'Yes, but then Viktor Novak would still be the ruler of this world.'

'I understand,' Ren-*ya* said. 'You came back to the caves for revenge.'

'No, I came back for you.'

Ren-*ya* shrugged, but she looked pleased. 'I would have been all right.'

Bela smiled. 'If anyone could've found a way to escape, it would've been you. *I* wouldn't have been all right though.'

'Why not? You could have been happy, with your father, your family.'

'You're my family, Ren-*ya*. I made a promise. We both did.' Bela held up her tattoo-marked hand. Ren-*ya* did the same, and they clasped their palms together.

'You must come back with me,' Bela said. 'You and all the Last who remain.'

Before Ren-*ya* could reply, a shadow fell over them and Bela turned to see Eagle standing in the entrance to the cave. 'That cannot be,' she said. 'There is no place for Ren-*ya* and her people in your world.'

Bela shook her head. 'But the prophecy says the descendants of the Last will return.'

Eagle's tawny eyes met Bela's. 'And they shall.'

Bela felt Ren-*ya*'s hand on her shoulder. 'It's you, *suran-ya*,' she said. 'The blood of our mother, of all our people, runs through your veins. You are one of us. You are the one, the descendant who will return and fulfil the prophecy.'

'But it's not fair,' Bela said to Eagle. 'I've only just found my sister, and you're telling me I have to leave her?'

'I am sorry for both of you,' Eagle said. 'But it is what must be.'

'So I'll grow up in the waking world, while she ʼins here, a child forever?'

344

'It does not have to be so.' Eagle raised one feathered eyebrow. 'Tonight is the black night, the darkest night. On this last night of the year, those who have survived the *long winter* return to their people to become full members of their clan.'

Ren-*ya* let out a great sigh. 'I have seen so many of these last nights, but each time the new moon comes and I am still a child.'

'There is a way, Ren-*ya*,' Eagle said. 'But it can only be done with *suran-ya's* help.'

Bela squeezed Ren-*ya's* hand. 'Ask me anything and I'll do it.'

'But there is no *smoke* for the ceremony,' Ren-*ya* said. 'The spirits will not come.'

'Selfless acts shall be rewarded.' Eagle placed a hand on Ren-*ya's* bowed head. 'I will make you a new *smoke*. Tonight we will carry out the ceremony, and afterwards *suran-ya* will sleep and return to her own world.'

She turned to Bela. 'Show me the totem.'

Bela took the orb from her parka and held it up.

Eagle peered into the brightness of the stone. 'Do you see the light within? Your home is there. You hold the whole waking world in your hand.'

'How can that be?' Bela said.

'It is a magical thing,' Eagle replied. 'When you

pass between the worlds, the totem turns inside out. The world it holds inside emerges, while it swallows down the world you came from.

'Our worlds have reflected each other across the ages,' Eagle continued. 'Like the stars that seem to float on the surface of a clear forest pool. But when you return home, you must destroy the totem. This will be the ripple that breaks the reflection. The whispers between the worlds will be silenced, and our time will begin to move on.'

'But . . . then I'll never be able to return,' Bela said. 'Ren-*ya* and I will never see each other again.'

'Not as living spirits,' Eagle said. 'But the dead do not need the totem in order to enter the spirit world. At the end of your life, your body will be laid in the earth. Your spirit will fly here like a bird and join the spirits of your mother and your sister, of all your people. Your children too will come here, and their children, and your descendants ever after, since they will all carry the blood of the Last.'

Ren-*ya* turned to Bela. 'You see, *suran-ya*? Nothing is forever. The guardian spirits are wise and good.'

Eagle left the girls alone to prepare for the ceremony that night.

Together, they painted a triangle of ochre dots on all of the cave. Together, they bowed their heads and whispered to the spirits: *the arrowhead of the hunter, the wing of the bird that passes between the worlds, the mountain in whose shadow we all live.*

Bela gazed at her sister. 'I wonder,' she said. 'What will you do when you grow up?'

'I will do what Malor once did for me,' Ren-*ya* said. 'I will teach the children how to fight, how to survive. After all, no one knows how to live through the *long winter* better than I do.

'And you?' She turned to Bela. 'What will you do in your world?'

Bela thought of Arno loyally watching over her as she slept. She thought of Eva who would be waiting for her return. 'I will continue my father's work.'

'I think Mam would be proud of us both,' Ren-*ya* said.

UNDER THE BLAZING STARS

That night they built a roaring fire in a clearing at the foot of the mountain.

'We must summon the spirits,' Eagle said. She took the ashes she had collected from the fire in the Cave of the Spirits and ground them to a fine powder on a flat stone. 'Give me your knife,' she said to Bela. 'The one Nagar made from the bone of a killer whale.'

Eagle cut a long wound in her palm. 'My blood shall stand for all the blood of the Last.' She held her hand over the stone, and let her blood drip on to the ashes. She mixed them together with the blade of knife and scraped the mixture into the fire. ky purplish haze filled the clearing.

'Breathe,' Eagle commanded. 'Breathe in the *smoke* and the ancestors will come.'

Bela filled her lungs. For a moment, a deep hush lay across the forest and then the silence was broken by the sound of many beating wings.

Although the *smoke* swirled thickly round her, Bela's vision was sharper than it had ever been and her gaze penetrated the darkness. She could see up into the night sky, where a host of birds with glowing eyes were gathering under the blazing stars.

One by one they came to land in the tall trees at the edge of the clearing. There were vultures, hawks and fish eagles, ravens as dark as the night and owls with round golden eyes. There were tiny birds with tawny feathers and blood-red chests. But Bela's eye was drawn to only one. Despite the darkness, she could see the flash of the magpie's black-and-white plumage in the night. The bird flew down to perch on Bela's shoulder and rubbed its glossy head against her cheek.

'Step forward, *suran-ya*,' Eagle said. 'You must be the one to crown her.'

Bela went and stood in front of Ren-*ya*. 'I will never forget you,' Bela said. 'You have taught me who I am, and what I can become. For the rest of my life, I will say your name.'

She placed the pine-frond crown she'd made on Ren-*ya*'s head. 'I will remember you as Ren,' she said. 'For tomorrow you won't be Ren-*ya* any more.'

Ren-*ya* looked up at her and they linked their fingers, clasped their living hands together for the last time.

Bela seemed to see the whole world as she gazed into her sister's eyes. Everything was there: the bird on her shoulder, the spirits in the trees, the fire and the starry night. She saw herself, and who she was, reflected in her sister's black eyes.

EPILOGUE
Kraków, 1912

Bela peeped out from behind the heavy velvet curtain at the edge of the stage. Every seat in the auditorium was taken and the room buzzed with excited chatter. She could see Arno wearing his brand-new suit in the middle of the front row.

'There are so many people here,' she said.

Eva swallowed and smoothed down her dress. 'I have to admit, I feel a little nervous.'

'So do I,' Bela said. 'But think how proud my father would be.'

At that moment, a man stepped on to the stage and took his place at the podium. 'Good evening, colleagues and friends. As President of the Copernicus Society of Naturalists, it is my great pleasure and privilege to welcome you to this extraordinary lecture.

'No doubt you will have seen the frenzy of interest in the newspapers. You will have read something of this important work and wondered at the intriguing central hypothesis.'

He bowed his head. 'You will remember our esteemed colleague Alexander Novak. We were greatly saddened by his death, but it is some relief that his body has at last been found and he has been laid to rest alongside his beloved wife.

'Yet tonight he lives again. We are to hear from the two remarkable scientists – his assistant and his daughter – who have taken his work to new heights. You may be shocked that these pioneers are women, one no more than a girl.' Bela and Eva glanced at each other and rolled their eyes. 'Certainly, no female has ever before been invited here to speak. But this work is so insightful, so painstakingly researched, it deserves our rapt attention.'

He paused for dramatic effect. 'And now I will make you wait no longer. May I present the toast of the scientific world, Bela Novak and Eva Balinsky!'

At the mention of their names, the audience got to their feet and the room erupted in deafening applause.

As Bela, and Eva at her side, stepped out on to the stage, the image of Ren-*ya* as Bela had last seen her flashed into her mind. Only now she would be Ren:

an adult, a hunter and a warrior.

There was to be no mention in the lecture of Ren or the totem or the spirit world. How could there be? Who would ever believe Bela? She had broken the totem as soon as she returned and no living spirit would ever be able to cross between the worlds again. But now Bela pressed her tattooed hand to her heart and remembered her sister. All of this was for her; every word she'd written was for Ren.

'For many years now,' Bela began, 'we have known that we were not the first people to walk this earth. Yet we have believed in our superiority. We believed the ancestors who came before us were little more than beasts. But now there is much evidence that our forebears were highly intelligent. Look at this.' She nodded to Eva, who held up the white stone carving of the lion-headed man. The audience gasped.

Bela went on to display some of the other artefacts her father had found: a beautifully carved bone rattle that showed how the people of the past had loved their children; the burial goods that revealed their belief in the afterlife, their reverence for the dead; the healed bones that proved the sick had been cared for.

'They were not so unlike us,' Bela continued. 'They too were artists and scientists. They too had beliefs, customs, culture. They loved and fought, laughed and cried. There is far more to discover, and all of it is just waiting to be found, buried in the ice beneath our feet.'

Acknowledgements

T he first spark of an idea for *The Ice Whisperers* came to me almost ten years ago. I have lost count of the number of times since then that it has been rewritten, reimagined, rewritten again. It languished in a drawer for years at a time. But there was something about it that kept calling me back. I would see a new way of making it work, get the manuscript out and start writing it all over again. My thanks go to all the people who helped me persevere on the journey:

To my inspirational Bath Spa University tutors, Steve Voake and Julia Green, who enabled me, and so many others, to develop the skills and confidence to write for children.

To the talented MA group who introduced me to the joy of being part of a community of writers, Pat Robson, Kim Lloyd, Ekwy Nnene, Jemma Hathaway, Sarah Waterstone and Cerianne Teague, and those who are part of my current writing community and who have read, critiqued, commiserated, celebrated and helped me with this story in so many ways: Nicola Lush, Eugene Lambert, Lu Hersey and Val Mote.

To my wonderful agent, Jo Williamson, whose enthusiastic YES meant so much and who is the best champion a children's author could have.

To my amazing editor, Emma Jones, who finds the path between the woods and the trees, who loves Bela and Ren-*ya* as much as I do and helped me uncover and deepen the emotional story between the sisters.

To all the talented people who make up the Puffin team, and who know exactly how to make a book as enticing as it can be.

To the super-talented Marco Guadalupi for the gorgeous cover and beautiful illustrations.

To my son, Joe, for giving my plot ideas the time of day, and my stepson, Leon, for technical advice and mythological chat. To Alli, Anna, David, Laura, Lucy, Ray, Remi and Sally for their friendship, belief and support. And especially to my husband, Kat, my first reader and critical friend.

Finally, to Mum, who is greatly missed, and who taught me to read and love books.

About the Author

Helenka Stachera grew up in a yellow-brick house in the woods with her British mother and Polish father, which stoked her lifelong obsession with fairy tales and legends. A Bath Spa graduate who now lives in Bristol with her husband, Helenka wrote her magical debut novel *The Ice Whisperers* to explore themes of family and belonging that, as an adopted daughter, are very close to her heart.